ONE MORE YEAR

A Pedro the Water Dog Saves the Planet Primer

AVIS KALFSBEEK

EXTRA FUN READS!

FREE DOWNLOAD

3 SHORT STORY PREQUELS:

Bird-Bully Besties

Lucky Mustard

Giro di Baci

Acknowledgments:
Patron Patrons ~ Benjamin Katz Creative
City of Sandpoint ~ Elio Longobardi
Patrick Gordis ~ Seattle (206) Bike Polo

ISBN 978-1-7355613-1-8 (First Edition Hardback)
ISBN 978-1-7355613-2-5 (First Edition Paperback)
ISBN 978-1-7355613-0-1 (Ebook)

www.AvisKalfsbeek.com

❀ Created with Vellum

For Jessie Elizabeth and Timothy Moore

CHAPTER 1

A.E. NELSON 1959 FISHING CREEL WICKER BASKET WITH LEATHER STRAP

High above sea level and within a blink of a peace-loving country, a narrow handle of a state contains one of the deepest, most beautiful, glacier-formed lakes in the world. On a warm late spring afternoon, in a modern time when many say the earth will eventually not sustain human life, a strong swimmer pulls a paddleboard on a crystal clear lake, surrounded by steep, craggy mountains. Her curly black-haired dog sits regally at the front of the board. The silence of the lake amplifies the rhythmic sounds of her stroke and breath.

"P, your turn!"

Pedro, known affectionately by Tilly as "P," becomes alert, takes a few steps back and forth on the paddleboard as Tilly swims up and kisses him on the snout. Pedro leaps off the front, swims to find the harness, and takes it in his mouth. Tilly's smooth, black long hair shimmers on her back in the sunshine as she pulls herself up strongly onto the board and attaches the harness to the joyous dog.

"Let's go, handsome," she says lovingly, then commands, "P, go!"

Pedro happily pulls Tilly as she kneels on the board in a meditative pose with the sun now low on the lake, their ujjayi and canine breaths melding.

"P, stop. Come!"

Pedro swims quickly back and Tilly lifts him onto the board. "Go aft. Sit!"

Pedro reluctantly walks to the rear of the board and sits, whimpering a little, then a lot, wanting to be closer. Tilly pulls a weight out of a vintage fishing basket, ties it to a rope and throws it into the water to anchor the boat. The water dog, accustomed to diving and retrieving objects underwater from the generations of fishing dogs in his ancestry, moves to jump in after it.

"No, P. Stay. Good boy."

Flowing smoothly through a series of yoga moves on the board as P watches, Tilly finishes standing in prayer pose, looks at her dog with a loving sparkle in her eye, pauses to enjoy his building excitement, then calls out, "Play!"

In unison, they dive off the board and swim as fast as they can in a friendly race. Tilly looks up at Pedro, laughs, then swims faster to beat him and circles back. She climbs up onto the board and pulls him up too, giving him a big wet hug as he pants happily in her arms.

Pedro barks suddenly. Tilly notices they have floated within sight of the shore of a small island, the anchor not having reached the bottom of the deep lake.

"What do you see?"

Pedro continues to bark and pace anxiously.

"Stay P. I don't see what you see." Tilly looks around. "Oh well, let's go. It's getting late."

Tilly paddles towards the marina as Pedro paces, keeping an eye back on the shore, eventually sitting at the front of the board like a figurehead on an ancient ship. A chocolate

Labrador jumps into the water to swim after them. She quickly realizes they are too far away, turns back, shakes off at shore, and runs up a trail that leads from the beach up into the woods.

CHAPTER 2
WHITE 1978 TOYOTA LONGBED PICKUP TRUCK

Tilly paddles along the shore towards the marina. She and Pedro float by a small, two-room log cabin where flower boxes sit under the front windows, and a bicycle rests on the porch alongside a basket filled with herbs waiting to be planted. A bit further down the shoreline, a gargantuan structure of logs towers over the surrounding trees. Tilly counts twenty-eight windows on the front of the three-story log house. It has a wrap-around porch and boat dock with a guest house beside it larger than Tilly's cottage. There are three SUVs, one luxury sedan, four jet skis, two touring motorcycles, and a thirty-eight-foot travel trailer in the driveway.

Burr, a lanky teenager, pumps gas into an old, funky houseboat with a pirate flag. The boat belongs to Ike, a tan leather-skinned man with tattoos and a white beard, dressed in khaki shorts without a shirt.

"Look, Ike, it's Tilly!" Burr's face lights up as he tries to look busy and important.

"I see them," he says grumpily. "Look at you, all puffed up like a peacock on huckleberries. Settle down, Burr. You'll get gas on yourself and blow up like a firecracker when you light your joint after work."

Burr ignores him and gives Tilly a big smile as she and Pedro approach the dock.

"Here's a spot, Tilly! I think P likes it over here."

Pedro jumps onto the dock with Burr's help and gives him a lick. Burr exuberantly pets him, never looking away from Tilly.

"Thanks, Burr. How's it going?" Tilly takes his hand and steps onto the dock. Burr pulls her board out of the water.

"I'm good. Caught some fish this morning. Would you like to come over for dinner? My mom could cook them for us."

"Oh, thank you, but I can't tonight. I should send P out with you sometime. He loves to help with fishing."

Burr tries to hide his disappointment with a weak smile.

"Hi, Ike! I see you've got your boat going for the season. Nice!"

"Yeah, it was a long cold winter but she started right up! Is this young man bothering you?" Ike scowls at Burr.

"No. Thanks though Ike. I'll let you know if he does." Tilly smiles at both of them.

"Hey Ike, did you see happen to see the logging trucks on Blue Lightning when you were out riding? That seems so close to town. What's up with that?"

"No, I didn't. I'll try to see who's up there and where exactly. Greedy pillaging bastards."

"Thanks. I was especially concerned because the road they were coming out of is very close to the sacred grounds. I didn't have P with me when I saw them -- he was doing his rounds at the Mountain Rest Home, the folks there love him -- and I was nervous to go in by myself."

"I'm on it."

Tilly hugs Ike. "Thanks."

Burr gives her a what-about-me puppy look, so she hugs

him too and smiles. Burr looks up to the heavens with a smile.

Tilly picks up her board. "Let's go, P." She loads it into the long bed of her old white Toyota pickup truck and opens the driver's side door.

"Load up!"

Pedro jumps quickly into the truck, moves over to the passenger side and puts his head out the window. Tilly waves goodbye to Burr and Ike as she drives off.

CHAPTER 3
SKY BLUE LINEN 1984 BUTTON-DOWN BROOKS BROTHERS SHIRT

Morning light streams through the kitchen window the next day as Tilly makes a smoothie and Pedro paces anxiously at her feet. She opens a locket hanging around her neck, looks at it with a pause, closes it, and kisses it gently. Pedro paws at the front door, then nudges the paddleboard and barks.

"No, P. It's a mountain day."

He barks again.

"We went swimming yesterday, remember? Why do you have to swim today?"

Tilly bends down to hold his head, her face close to his. "Because you are Pedro de Sousa Saramago Magellan, and every ounce of your doggie DNA needs to be in the water, right?"

Tilly turns to put a dish in the sink, and when she turns back around Pedro gives her his most convincing puppy eyes.

"Don't give me those eyes. I read that you dogs do that on purpose to manipulate people. Well, it works. You!"

Tilly hugs him then grabs her phone from the counter.

"I'll tell Camas we're water doggin' it today. She won't be happy."

Tilly and Pedro swim and play in the lake. They practice retrieving a weighted baton. Tilly throws it, he reaches it and then bumps it under the water again and again with his nose, so the game of fetch is never-ending.

Pedro suddenly stops his game, barks and excitedly swims off.

"P, come. P, stay!" Tilly calls.

Pedro swims quickly towards the island they had seen the day before.

"P! Come!" she repeats. "P! Return to ship! Shit!"

Pedro bounds out of the water onto the shore and shakes himself off as the chocolate Lab kisses his face and turns to run up the trail. He follows her, disappearing into the woods.

Tilly docks the paddleboard and follows them up a steep, meandering trail through tall bushes and wildflowers. She hears a hawk call overhead and recognizes that as a sign of something, but she does not know what.

"P, come! P!"

Tilly runs fast up the very steep last stretch. She arrives at the top a bit winded, pausing with her hands on her thighs. She walks through an arbor with vines, which leads to a quaint old cottage, overgrown with climbing rose bushes, with a porch and red front door. The surrounding air has the rich almond-clove smell of lilac bushes.

Tilly can hear Pedro barking, not in a fearful way, but in an I'm-so-excited-and-where-are-you-Tilly kind of way. He and his new friend run out from behind the cottage and race up to Tilly. She laughs in relief and pets them both, as a man bursts out the door onto the front porch. Graeme Selkirk is ruggedly handsome, with tan skin and deep crows feet around his blue eyes. He has a scruffy beard, longish blonde-grey hair, and wears a well-made but lightly frayed blue linen shirt, shorts and no shoes. The peeling paint on the well-constructed cottage seems to match the demeanor of its owner, both weathered survivors.

"What are you doing here?" Graeme says in a firm, low voice. "This is a private island. Didn't you see the signs?"

Surprised at his unfriendly tone, Tilly responds defiantly, "No, I didn't actually. My dog heard your dog barking, and I came looking for him."

"It is private." His tone now softening a little, "You better get back. Those skies look dark over there. I'll walk you back to the dock."

As they walk toward the path to go down, Tilly notices a rustic deck platform overlooking the lake with a metal frame on top of it. Pedro runs up and sniffs around it.

"What's that thing, if you don't mind me asking?"

"I do mind, actually."

"Well, aren't you a man of mystery."

Graeme grunts. "And you're a trespasser, so pardon me if I don't give you a tour, water princess."

"I was just curious."

"Well, you can be curious about someone or something else, somewhere else. Be on your way now," Graeme says seriously as he motions to the path down.

Graeme grimaces as he starts to walk down the hill. He puts his hand on his thigh.

At the bottom of the hill, Pedro jumps on the paddleboard, and the chocolate Lab follows, sitting as close as she can to him. Tilly catches Graeme with a small smile. He quickly turns serious again.

"Come along, Roxie."

Roxie doesn't budge, sitting very happily with Pedro.

He calls more loudly. "Roxie, now! Come!"

Roxie kisses Pedro with a lick, whimpers, and jumps off the paddleboard onto the dock. Graeme walks briskly with a small limp up the trail, and Roxie follows.

Tilly gets onto the board and pushes off with her paddle towards the marina. After several strokes, she looks back toward the island with concern.

"Well, he was certainly grumpy. I hope he's nicer to Roxie than he was to us."

Pedro barks in agreement.

Tilly pets him, then paddles away from the island.

CHAPTER 4
OAK-HANDLED 61 INCH LONG
1943 FISHING NET

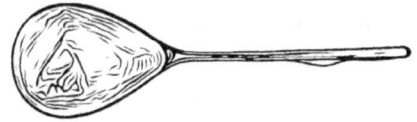

The next morning, the sounds of Led Zeppelin from Ike's houseboat ripple loudly over the shimmering lake water. Ike sits reading in his chair on the deck. Stacks and stacks of books surround his chair and fill the boat's cabin.

A scraggly, old black cat saunters around the boat until he sees a bird land lightly on the bow. He crouches down and slowly stalks along towards the bird. The bird flies to the adjacent houseboat, a similarly ancient, funky vessel with a diving board on the deck. The cat pounces to the neighboring boat, with claws out, ready to grasp the bird. He miscalculates, his momentum too great to stop, and skids off the edge of the vessel into the water.

Ike hears the splash, looks up from his book, and stands up. "Suerte, not again!" he exclaims as he shakes his white beard.

He grabs a long-handled fishing net and scoops the dripping wet, scrawny cat out of the water. He deposits Suerte on the deck and grabs a towel.

"Come here, ya ol' cat." He grabs the cat by the scruff of

his neck, wraps the towel around him on his lap, and dries him off lovingly.

"Listen, Suert. You're already on your eighth life, so you need to take it easy, man. One of these days, I'm not going to see you go over."

He lets Suerte go, and the cat slinks off to curl up in a sunny spot on the deck.

Ike sits to read his book in the sun. After a good hour, he reaches over to feel a dry cat and says, "Let's go see Bear."

Suerte jumps up and runs down into the cabin and curls up on Ike's bed. Ike starts the engine and pulls out of the slip onto the lake.

CHAPTER 5

CHOUINARD EQUIPMENT 1972
RED BACKPACK

Tilly runs up a steep mountain trail followed by her best friend, Camas, and Pedro. Pedro veers off the path back and forth to chase chipmunks and squirrels and bark at low-flying birds in the woods. Tilly reaches an overlook at the top of Amber Hill. Camas arrives almost a full minute after her friend, very winded, her freckled face flush. Camas is strong, athletically built, with an artistically tattooed sleeve on her left arm. She has curly red hair, and some might label her full-figured. She wears a Dead Kennedys T-shirt and sporty bright colors.

"What the fungus?! Damn, Tilly. Slow the hell down, girl. I thought you said we were going to hike today, and then you run the whole way. Don't you ever stop to smell the pine needles?!"

"Yes, I do. I smell them as I run past them."

"Oh, you do, do you?" Camas says with a smile. "I think you're going so fast you can't see or smell a damn thing. Where's P?"

"Oh, gosh. P!"

"See, you lost your damn dog!"

Pedro races up the last part of the hill to the edge of the rocks at the lookout, nearly falls off, then turns around and licks Camas' hand.

"What's your T-shirt? OMY? I was going to ask you earlier, but we couldn't even have a conversation because you were racing, not trail running."

"It's a project I'm working on."

They sit down on a large, flat rock overlooking the lake. Tilly pulls some fruit, bread and cheese out of her backpack and sets them out on a large, colorful cloth napkin.

"Mmmm, yum... I want to hear more, but first, let's have a beer."

Camas grabs a couple of Laughing Dog IPA's from her backpack and opens them quickly with a beer opener hanging from her pack. She puts her mouth over the escaping beer foam, first one, then the other.

Tilly laughs, "You can't go anywhere without drinking, can you? That cold beer does look perfect though, especially paired with this Manchego."

"Yep, beer is one of the five basic food groups."

"You have five? I would have guessed fewer. Beer and?"

"Pizza, ice cream, huckleberries and cannabis."

Tilly laughs, shaking her head, "I think you are one of the strongest people I know despite the questionable things you put in your body."

Camas flexes her impressive bicep in the air with the beer in her hand. "Food rewards the watts. Why else would we suffer?" She takes a drink, "So, what's the project?"

Tilly looks out over the lake and is quiet. Finally, she says, "Sometimes when I see the coal cars passing over the lake on the train tracks day after day, I feel so helpless."

"What's the big deal? We need that coal to make the cities light up, right?"

Tilly pulls her beanie down over her eyes to hide her tears.

She keeps it there and continues slowly, "Did you know that they chop the tops of mountains off to get to that coal, and they don't put them back?"

Camas puts her arm around her. "Oh, you sensitive twit. I love your passion. I prefer passion for handsome guys. Thank goodness the earth has you."

Tilly pushes the cap up, tears still in her eyes, and smiles at her friend.

"So, O M Y stands for *one more year*. I had a dream, about a month ago, about the Crying Indian."

Camas looks confused.

"You know, from the public service announcement in the 70s that tried to get people to stop littering and polluting. We're too young to remember, but the roadsides across the country were a dump full of litter back then," Tilly explains patiently.

"*Indian* is not PC," Camas teases.

"I think the dream was telling me that we need another PSA to curb our overconsumption. That's One More Year."

"Huh?" Camas grunts with her mouth full.

"People should keep their stuff longer. Don't just go get a new cell phone because you're eligible, don't lease a new car because you can afford the payment, don't buy that new outfit because you're depressed and bored."

"I just did all three of those things this month! What's wrong with that?"

Tilly doesn't laugh.

"You know I'm kidding, but I did think about doing those things."

"I know, I won't change you overnight. God knows I've been trying for years, but if you just wait for one more year on one of those things, and your neighbor does too, and your mother, and her neighbor, it might slow down the zombie wastefulness."

Tilly's voice becomes louder and louder. "Even our energy-efficient cars have batteries that come from water-polluting lithium and copper mines. We need to slow this all down!"

Pedro raises his head from sleeping and barks.

"Sold! Where can I get my T-shirt?"

Tilly smiles broadly, pleased, "I'll make you one tonight."

They pack up their picnic, walk into the woods and squat down to pee, their faces looking out over the bushes.

"I meant to tell you I met a strange man and his dog on Opal Island yesterday. He was grumpy and unhappy."

"You be careful. Could be some weirdo out there."

"No. He was unusual, but I don't think he was a weirdo."

They pull up their shorts and walk to the trail.

"Love you, sista" Camas says.

"Love you too, friend."

The two hug. Tilly and Pedro take off running.

"Slow your skinny butt down!"

CHAPTER 6

FEUER WEAR 2017 RECYCLED FIRE HOSE MESSENGER BAG

A small seaplane, with classical music playing through its headsets, flies over several tiny islands in Lake Bijou Nez. The conversation of two men, Jimmy, a stocky red-haired pilot in his thirties, and Bill, in his sixties, a portly man with a well-groomed salt and pepper beard, talk over the music.

"That's it, Jimmy."

"Yes, I know, sir. But thank you," he says respectfully, with a slight Southern drawl.

The plane lands on the water and docks. Roxie races down the path from the cottage and out onto the dock to greet the aircraft.

Bill, dressed in a white polo shirt, blue and white seer-sucker pants, white bucks, a Panama hat and sunglasses, steps out of the plane and grabs a messenger bag made from recycled firehose from behind the cockpit.

"Thanks, Jimmy. I should only be a couple of hours, then we'll head back to Spokane. No beer until we're back home."

"Yes, sir."

Bill answers his cell phone, "I know, I know. What am I

doing here? Because if I don't come to see you, I'll never see you. That's why. Don't go hide in the wilderness. I'll be right there, so you might as well get started fixing me lunch."

Bill makes it to the top of the path, panting heavily. "When are you going to put a gondola on that godforsaken hill?"

"Come on in, you fat old son of a badger," Graeme says with a smile, as he embraces him in a firm hug. "I don't have much, but I'll throw something together."

The patio table overlooking the lake is filled with colorful vegetables, cheeses, a couple of salads, crusty bread, olive oil in a vintage Italian dispenser and a bottle of red wine.

"Not too shabby for throwing something together. It looks like you were expecting me."

Graeme laughs. The two eat and drink for several minutes in silence.

After a bit of wine, Bill blurts, "Graeme, what in the world are you doing here? You're in the middle of nowhere, with no human interaction."

"Who needs humans when I have Roxie?" Graeme pets Roxie, and she licks his hand.

"Seriously. I'm worried about you."

"You worried? How could a man with more money than god and a beautiful wife have a worry in the world? By the way, I do get some human interaction. Why just yesterday, I was visited by a young woman and her dog."

"Did you speak with her or just shoot cannonballs at her boat?"

"Very funny. No cannonballs. We spoke."

Bill sees Graeme's trainer.

"Are you training?"

"Why would I train?" Graeme says with a pained face.

"Because you love it?"

"That was a past life," he says sternly. Graeme looks away.

"I told your mother I'd look out for you when she passed away."

Graeme continues eating without a response.

"I don't want to spoil this beautiful lunch. Let's change the subject. How about Edmonton taking the cup this year?"

"Those bastards," Graeme says dryly.

CHAPTER 7
MARIN PALISADES TRAIL 1993
MOUNTAIN BIKE

Ike arrives at an old dock, nestled in a wooded area with a beautiful emerald bay and a scattering of tent campers. He ties up the boat, then pops his head into the cabin to let Suerte know he is going to leave.

"Stay put, Suert. Shred any trespassers, tiger."

He unties an old mountain bike from the boat and lifts it out onto the dock. He steps off the boat, flips a wood sign around from, *No, I'm not friendly*, on one side to, *If you step on my boat, my guard cat will attack you*.

He puts his leg over the bike and lets out an old-man groan, "Shit, I'm too old for this."

Ike rides briskly down the trail, rusty at first, but as he goes up and then down a small hill, he feels muscles loosen, tendons relax, and he smiles joyfully. He sees a small stream ahead with a human-made jump just in front of it. He contemplates his options, gains speed, and jumps the stream, landing smoothly on the other side.

"Whoop!! I've still got it!" he yells loudly into the quiet forest.

Ike continues on the trail through the woods and comes

upon a simple log cabin. Frida, a pretty older woman with deep set wrinkles on her face and long grey hair, is standing outside.

"Ike, is that you?" Frida calls as he rides up. She gives him a strong hug.

"Frida. You look radiant as usual."

"Oh Ike, you're such a charmer. How's Suerte?"

"Same ol', same ol'. Near-death experiences daily."

Frida chuckles. "You lookin' for Bear?"

"Yeah, he around? I have a question about some logging nearby."

"He's fishing, but he promised to be back by lunch. Let me make you a coffee. Can you stay to have lunch with us?"

"Of course."

Frida goes into the cottage to start lunch. Ike sits his tired body down on an old porch swing outside, watching for Bear.

CHAPTER 8
DARIO PEGORETTI-BUILT 1994 PINARELLO ROAD BIKE

Roxie stands next to Graeme's bed, lays her chin down on the edge of the mattress, and watches him sleep. The sun rises a bit higher, and the light streams into the austere room furnished with quality bedding on a turn-of-the-century, wooden bed frame, a nightstand and a dresser. A vintage cycling photo hangs on the wall of Gino Bartali with some other cyclists circa 1930's Tour de France.

Roxie walks into the closet and drags an old duffel bag out onto the floor. She whimpers a bit and then lets out a bark. Graeme rolls over as she jumps onto the bed.

"You just can't let me sleep, can you?" he says as he grabs her to scratch her neck.

Graeme gets out of bed a bit groggy and trips on the bag.

Frustrated and confused, he raises his voice, "Damn it, Roxie!"

His sleepy eyes focus in to see the bag.

"What's this, girl?" he says more calmly.

He unzips the bag and pulls out a cycling shoe.

"Silly dog."

Graeme walks into the kitchen, puts the shoe on the counter, and starts to make coffee. Roxie pulls the other shoe out of the bag and brings it to him, bumping it onto his hand. Graeme shakes his head and then looks outside.

"Well, maybe just today."

Graeme walks out in just his boxer shorts to a corrugated metal shed behind the cottage. He sits down on the stairs and puts on the cycling shoes. He takes a 1990's-era road bicycle out of the shed, grabs a bike pump, and inflates the tires. There are somehow no holes.

"That's a small miracle."

He walks the bike over to the metal frame contraption that Tilly had asked him about, puts the bike on top of it, and gets on. Graeme clips on and begins spinning, riding in place on the trainer. He lets out a loud groan, speaking in the distinct languages of Italian and age, as his past injuries scream to make themselves known. He pushes through and continues to spin.

Roxie barks excitedly.

Graeme smiles at her. "Well, aren't you just so proud of yourself."

Graeme rides for several minutes, then slows down. The past encroaches on his mind, putting his feet on the bicycle pedals into thick mud. Pained more by his thoughts than tight muscles and the metal pins that hold some parts of him together, he spins slower and slower.

Roxie barks again. Then again.

Graeme suddenly revives, lifting his head to look out over the lake. He pedals faster and faster, then gets up out of the saddle to stand on the pedals, spinning faster and harder now. Roxie keeps a close watch.

Finally exhausted, he slows and then comes to a stop. Sweat drips from his body and face. Graeme stumbles off the trainer. He lifts the bike off and walks slowly to put it back in the shed. Roxie licks at his perspiring legs.

He turns, and Roxie follows him to the house. Graeme rests the bike outside the front door on the porch. He leans down and pets Roxie.

"Good girl."

CHAPTER 9

BIRMINGHAM STOVE & RANGE 1967 CAST IRON DUTCH OVEN NO. 7

Down the shadowed forest trail, a silhouette of a large figure approaches the log cabin. As he comes through the trees and emerges into the sunlight, Bear, 6'5", looks bigger than a linebacker. He has long black hair and wears old jeans, boots, and a well-worn flannel shirt with rolled-up sleeves. Black ink, in an art-culture blend of Day of the Dead to Native American to Samoan, cover his forearms. His large horse carries his fishing bag, pole and a bundle of freshly caught trout.

Bear smiles broadly when he sees Ike, his 67 years not showing in the sparkle of his brown eyes or smooth skin. "Ike! My friend."

Bear gives Ike an enthusiastic hug, lifting him off the ground. He sets him down and bends over to look at him closely, six inches from his face. "You look a little serious."

"I came to ask for your help."

Frida comes out of the cabin with a tray of huckleberries, fresh bread, and goat cheese from the neighboring farm. "Bear, give me that fish, please. I'll cook some up on the fire."

She hands the tray to Ike, "and here are some things to start on."

"Oh, my favorite mustard! Thank you, Frida. You are a queen of queens," Ike says, taking the tray from her hands.

Frida rushes off to prepare more mountain and stream delicacies. Bear and Ike sit and eat a few bites quietly. Bear towers over Ike, even when seated.

"What do you need? You know I'll do whatever you ask."

"Tilly saw a logging truck coming out of Blue Lightning Road. It wasn't far from the sacred grounds. She was nervous to check it out herself, which is unusual for Tilly, she's not afraid of much, but those bastards can be mean, ya know?"

"Oh, Tilly, how is she?" Bear says gently.

"She's great. Swimming and running with that hairy black dog all the time."

"I'll ride over there tomorrow and let you know what I see."

"Thanks, buddy." Ike stands up and gives Bear another hug.

"When are you going to get rid of the boat and come live up here with us?"

"You know I can't live on land."

Frida walks up with a platter of beautifully barbecued trout and sautéed wild Morel mushrooms. "Here's your catch."

Frida sits, bows her head, and closes her eyes. Bear and Ike do the same. She blesses the food in her ancestor's language and adds, "I see that in this simple manner, The Great Spirit takes care of us."

She opens her eyes and smiles, "Did you solve the world's problems yet?"

"Almost," Ike says. "We just have one or two left. Like when are you going to leave this giant lug and come live on the boat with me?"

They laugh and continue their soul feast under the canopy of tall trees.

CHAPTER 10

KOSS 1975 EASY LISTENER STEREOPHONE HEADPHONES

A mountain montage reveals an old love rediscovered as spring gives way to summer. Outcrops of tall beargrass bloom and huckleberry bushes hide nibbling bear cubs.

Though Roxie accepts her master's girth, she hopes his dog-walking pace will improve. She barks impatiently at the foot of Graeme's bed. Graeme opens his eyes, shakes his head at Roxie, pulls on an ancient pair of college shorts and a threadbare T-shirt, fixes a coffee, and walks slowly out to the trainer to ride.

Across the lake, Tilly pulls Pedro, proudly holding a baton in his mouth, on the paddleboard. She stops, takes it from him, and throws it. Pedro leaps off the board into the clear water to retrieve it.

A colorful crew of skilled mountain bikers, Josh, Cutter, Joe and Reeve, affectionately called The Bike Guys, race down a winding, bermed, mountain bike trail. They joke and laugh as they pass Tilly and Camas running up the trail past them. The guys say, "hey," and give friendly nods. Josh shouts, "Nice old school headphones, Camas!"

As the sun struggles to peek over the horizon, Roxie jumps onto Graeme's bed with a cycling shoe in her mouth. With one eye open, Graeme lets out a dog-growl, "Grrrrrrrr."

Roxie's eyebrows lift.

He smiles at Roxie, gets out of bed with a spring in his step, makes a quick cup of coffee and heads out the door in shorts and a fifteen-year-old local Letera 22 Pub T-shirt. He grabs his bike, gets on the trainer, and energetically rides in place.

Tilly and Pedro pass a warning sign for Grizzly bears as they run along the wooded trail. They reach a waterfall overlook and peer out over the majestic view below. Pedro barks loudly at a Moose standing in the mist of the falls.

The Bike Guys race down a twisty lakeside trail, each of them standing on their pedals and deeply in tune with every rock and twig beneath their tires. When they reach the water, they pull foam floats out of their backpacks and tie them to their bikes. Taking turns, they ride down the bank and launch themselves from a wooden ramp out over the water. They each push their bike away in the air before pulling various dramatic gymnastic poses and comedic displays, splashing down, and swimming back to shore, bike in tow.

The next morning Roxie comes to Graeme's side of the bed as usual, though this time with a black garment in her mouth. She drops it on the comforter and licks Graeme's face. Graeme wakes, this morning without frustration.

"What have you found now, Roxie girl?"

He holds it up and sees they are cycling shorts. He pulls at them and notices threadbare areas and a hole.

"These have seen better days, haven't they, girl?"

Roxie barks.

"Yes, and so have I!" Graeme laughs.

Graeme puts on the shorts, goes outside, and climbs on his trainer. Roxie stands close by. Graeme cycles at a vigorous pace. With music pumping on his headphones, not at all winded, he looks out over the lake and smiles.

CHAPTER 11
MOTOROLA 1991 STAR-TAC FLIP MOBILE PHONE

Tilly paddles next to Ike's boat with Pedro firmly planted on the front of the board. Suerte comes up and purrs loudly in response to her caresses. Pedro is jealous and pushes his nose between the two. Suerte hisses and gives him a swat.

"Sorry, P. You need to stay."

Pedro lets out a whimper and curls up on the paddleboard.

"Hey, Suerte boy, where's Ike?" Suerte jumps down and uses his paw to open the cabin door. Ike comes out with a book in hand and reading glasses on, grumbling at Suerte for disturbing him.

"Oh, hello, Sunshine! How are you?" he says with a big smile.

"I'm great, Ike. What are you reading? Another boat story?"

"You got it. You know that's all I read. I decided several years ago that my boat and life could only accommodate nautical things. Nautical decor, nautical books, a nautical life. I'm rereading the Kon Tiki."

"I love that book. Especially the part where the fish are so plentiful they're leaping up onto the boat!"

"What a great description. And the challenges they went through. That's the type of man you need to find. One of those no-nonsense, whiny-free Nordic adventurers. Lars, or Dag or the like."

"If I did need to find a man, a no-nonsense type would be my preference. But I don't."

"I know, I know. But someday you need not swim so fast."

Tilly rolls her eyes.

"So, what brings you to the pirate ship... other than my charm and handsome good looks?"

Tilly laughs, then turns serious, "I came to visit, but I'm also curious if you heard anything about the logging trucks I saw the other day?"

"I went to see Bear. He and Frida fed me some delicious, freshly caught barbecued trout and cheese and bread and fresh-picked huckleberries and..." Ike reminisces dreamily of what other foods he had enjoyed. "Ummm... and some huckleberry pie with ice cream."

Ike pauses again, with a smile, thinking about the food.

"I rode my bike out there and, you know, I still have the moves. Took a jump and made the landing. Felt like I was Joe Breeze being chased by Gary Fisher, taking the Triple Ripple on Mt. Tam's Repack with speed and grace. It was awesome!" Ike is happily caught up in his food and bike dreaming.

Tilly waits respectfully, amused, then clears her throat, "Ike? What did Bear say?"

"Oh, sorry. He said that he would take a ride up there and check things out and let me know."

"Thanks, Ike."

Tilly's face is solemn now, as she looks towards the mountains. Suerte jumps into her lap.

"I brought you some things from Sandglass Books."

Ike's face lights up. "You did?!"

"Yup. All nautical."

Tilly hands Ike a paper bag.

"In the Heart of the Sea and The Floating Brothel."

"Thanks! I don't have either of those. I think I'll start the brothel book first!"

Ike opens the book and flips through some pages.

"I need to run. Text me when you hear from Bear," Tilly says, as she puts Suerte down and stands up.

"Text? I don't text. I have a flip phone from the 90s."

"How could that possibly still be working?"

"Well, it is still working," he says proudly. "Just like my 1960s boat and my 90s mountain bike. Just like the 1972 microwave that I won't let Suerte stand in front of. Just like my 1978 Honda three-wheeler motorcycle. Just like me!"

"I wish more people were like you. Keeping their stuff longer. It might just save this planet. When you hear from Bear, call me from that flip phone!"

"You got it!"

Tilly gets back onto her paddleboat with Pedro and pushes off the dock.

CHAPTER 12
NORTHERN OHIO BLANKET MILLS 1906 GREEN PLAID WOOL HORSE BLANKET

ear rides his tall Clydesdale through the woods to the sacred grounds where there is a grassy mound of earth in the middle of a meadow with wildflowers growing on top of it and a large, smooth oval stone. The area has other smooth stones in various places, and there is a fire circle made of rocks.

Bear dismounts and leads his horse to the edge of the small hill. He stops and closes his eyes as the breeze carries leaves and the fragrance of pine, musty moss, wild jasmine, and the orange blossom scent of Syringa into the air around him. Though perhaps the scent of jasmine flowers is left over from his earlier embrace with Frida.

Bear opens his eyes and turns to look toward the sound of saws in the distance. He gets back on his horse and rides into the woods. He quickly arrives to tall trees crashing to the ground, and groups of men loading logs with machinery onto semi-trucks. The sun bears down on the freshly cut stumps spread over the now stark, bare hillside.

One of the workers spots Bear riding up. He turns to the

foreman, a tall, stocky man, in his mid-fifties, with badly-dyed jet black hair, and points.

"Shit," the foreman says with a grimace.

Bear approaches on his horse.

"Bear, you better get off that horse, or he'll get spooked by the trucks."

"Gary. Looks like your busy pillaging the earth again. He's not spooked."

"This is loggin'. Not pillagin'."

"Where's your permit?"

"I don't need to show you no god damned permit, you son of a bobcat."

"Please don't use that kind of language around my horse."

"Go to hell, Bear. You've no business here."

"You're logging too close to the stream, and this hill's unstable. It's been that way since we played here as kids."

"We're fine. You get on out of here and mind your own damn business."

"It is my business when five hundred tons of soil and debris crash down on our sacred land. It'll be the town of Sandglass's business when it heads down the hill."

"I've got orders for eleven log homes. Not a single one under 10,000 square feet and the owners want to get underway yesterday. We need these logs now!"

Bear's head sinks and he closes his eyes.

He takes a breath, stands up straight, towering over Gary.

"It's a sad thing. A man spends his entire life sitting in a sterile office dreaming of coming to Montana or Sandglass, and when he finally retires, what does he do? Does he enjoy the land? Does he fish? Does he hike to find wild morels and huckleberries? Does he sit in a quiet kayak with his love? No, he spends the last precious years of his life building a 20,000 square foot ego palace with master suites on opposite ends, chopping down half the forest to do it, when he could have a wonderful life in a two-room cabin."

"Shove it, Bear!"

"Always the gentleman. Your mother, Aida, my godmother, would be so proud of the man who came back to town to be big rather than a part of things," Bear says with pity in his voice. "If you won't stop this, we'll get you shut down and removed from your position as Chief New Jeans."

The logger standing next to Gary turns away to hide his laughter. Bear leads his horse around to leave. Gary looks down at his dark denim jeans with an angry Trump-face frown. He walks up to a nearby truck and has the driver rev his engine.

Bear's horse doesn't flinch and calmly carries Bear back into the woods.

CHAPTER 13
25' 130 HP 1948 CLASSIC CHRIS-CRAFT SPORTSMAN

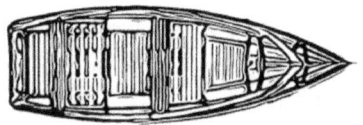

Graeme and Roxie climb into a 1940's wooden motorboat. Graeme is in shorts, a long-sleeved white linen shirt, and topsiders. He expertly navigates across the lake and up a nearby tributary. They travel up the stream, past kayakers, ducks, happy people floating in inner-tubes with coolers of beer, and the occasional otter. They arrive at a boat dock with a freshly mowed lawn and picnic tables in front of an old general store. Graeme ties up the boat and steps onto the dock. Roxie hops out behind him.

Graeme is nervous. "Roxie, are you with me?"

Roxie barks. They walk across the lawn into the store, and a young girl at the counter greets them. At the back of the store, an attractive slender woman with shoulder-length auburn hair with a few strands of grey, in her late forties, welcomes them with a double-take.

"Graeme? Roxie! "

"Hi, Liz. How are you?"

"I'm fine. I haven't seen you in twenty-six months. I've been worried."

"Bill has been bringing me provisions. I've become somewhat of a hermit."

"I see that," she says, smiling.

Graeme touches his long beard. "I need some things. Can you help me order them?"

"Sure. What do you need?"

"Here's my list. Whatever you don't have, I can come back for."

Liz looks over the list. "I have most of these. A few things I'll have to order. Like Roxie girl's special snacks. Is there anything else you ne..."

Graeme interrupts, "I need a kit."

"A kit?" she asks, surprised.

"Yes," Graeme says shyly, eyes diverted.

"That means your cycling again?"

"Well, I wouldn't say cycling. Just on the trainer with my "trainer" Roxie. She's relentless. Ever since I got on a few days ago, she won't leave me alone until I've trained each morning."

"Good girl, Roxie," Liz laughs.

"My old cycling clothes are rags."

"It's nice they still fit."

"Fit is a relative term."

"It's a bit of a coincidence, but do you happen to know the huge alpaca farm down the road?" Liz asks.

"Sure."

"Well, a fiber mill in Seattle is making knits for them. I've started a cycling line. Can I show you? If you hate it, you won't hurt my feelings."

Surprised, Graeme quickly says, "I'd love to see it. How did you start that?"

"It's the softest of soft, and I see all of the cyclists ride by my store and, well... you might or might not remember my dreams when we first met ..." Liz stops talking, looks at Graeme. "Did I hear you say you'd love to see it?"

"I'd love to see it."

Graeme watches Liz walk into the back room. She turns around and catches him looking at her. Liz turns away, keeps walking, and smiles to herself. She returns with a jersey and holds it up. It is light blue with black sleeves and collar and woven from lightweight alpaca fiber, with an emblem patch with the simple word *giro* on one shoulder.

Graeme touches the jersey. "Liz, this is fantastic. It looks like something from another era."

"I hope that's a compliment."

"It is."

"I don't have your size, but they'll be in by next week."

"I'll come back for it and the rest of the food supplies then. Do you have bike shorts?" Graeme asks.

"Don't laugh. They're traditional but with a soft alpaca lining."

"Who's laughing? I haven't had anything even close to my shorts in years. Two pairs, please!"

Liz laughs. Graeme puts his hand on top of hers.

"It's really great to see you," Graeme says softly.

Liz smiles at him, blushes, and looks away.

"Hey, Rox, let's let Liz get back to work."

They walk outside towards the boat.

Graeme turns around to face Liz. "Oh, I almost forgot. Do you know a girl with a black curly dog? She came onto the island, and I wasn't very nice to her, I'm afraid."

"That's Tilly."

"Tilly. OK, thanks. If you see her, will you apologize to her for me? After she left, I realized I was a grumpy ass."

"She's not the only one that left with hurt feelings."

"I know that," Graeme says solemnly. "I know."

Graeme and Roxie get into the boat.

"Don't be a stranger," Liz calls. She waves to them as the boat pulls away. Graeme waves back. Roxie barks.

CHAPTER 14
2003 MINI COOPER S WITH 303,311 MILES

Camas pulls up fast to the marina dock parking lot with music blaring from her red 2003 Mini Cooper. It has white racing stripes and a broken glovebox held up with matching red duct tape. She's singing along loudly to a fast-tempo, explicit rap song by the Red Hot Chili Peppers. She jumps out of her car and sees Burr standing on the dock.

"Hey, handsome. Where's Tilly?"

"Tilly? Tilly's here?"

"Don't ejaculate, jail bate. I'm just asking her whereabouts?"

"I haven't seen her."

"Shit. She told me she'd be here at six."

Camas hugs Burr. "Thanks, Buddy," she says and goes into the dockside restaurant bar.

"Kokanee, please."

"Sure thing," the bartender responds. "How ya doing today?"

"Great except my friend, the human Swiss watch, is late. She's never late. Better give me a shot of Cuervo too."

Camas looks at the time on her phone.

"You got it."

A dripping wet Pedro comes bounding into the bar.

"Hey, that dog will have to stay outside."

Pedro doesn't obey. He travels from Camas to the bartender, then to guests in the restaurant. Some are very happy to receive a wet kiss. Others, not so much.

Tilly rushes in, "P, come!"

Pedro runs to her, and she puts him on the leash.

"That's her, my better half," Camas says to the bartender, then, exasperated, to Tilly, "Where've you been?"

"Out on the lake."

"Out on the lake? That's a huge lake, and you've gone out on that godforsaken lake ever since I've known you, and you are never, never, ever late."

"Were you worried? I sense some worry," Tilly teases.

"Yes, I was worried!"

Camas takes a deep breath, followed by the shot of tequila. "Would you like some tequila?"

"Why not?"

"Two more shots of Cuervo and two Kokanee, please."

Camas downs her second shot and hands Tilly hers. Tilly takes a moderate sip. Camas grabs it from her and finishes it off, then suddenly wraps her arms around her friend in a firm hug. "Please don't do that to me again!"

Tilly hugs back. "I'll do my best. Let's go sit outside," she says as she walks towards the outdoor patio.

The two sit down at a table, and Pedro lies down at Tilly's feet. Tilly pulls a One More Year T-shirt out of her backpack and hands it to Camas.

"Thanks!"

Camas takes her T-shirt off. As she sits in her bra, feeling openly voluptuous, she glances around to see if any men are watching. None are. She shrugs and pulls the OMY T-shirt down over her head.

"Looks good!"

"It's cool. Thank you," Camas smiles, then says dryly, "So, what's new since this morning, when you canceled on me?"

"I'm sorry. You know that word 'doggedly'? Well, that's P. P for persistent."

Pedro's ears perk up when he hears his name. Camas rolls her eyes.

"I didn't do much out of the ordinary today." Tilly paused. "I've decided I'm going to do an Ironman."

Camas pretends to fall off her chair. "Whoa, Nellie," she says loudly. "Why the hell would you want to do that?"

Tilly shrugs.

"It looks majorly brutal, and you can't even cycle."

"I can ride a bike."

"Riding a bike and cycling are two different things. You don't even own a bike."

"I can get a bike."

"You need a real bike. Not some used, thrown together bike that will get you killed if it falls apart."

"We have the best bike surgeons in the world here in Sandglass. Reeve might fix me up."

"What about P? He's a water dog. Not a cycling dog."

"It's a triathlon. He swims and runs with me. I'm pretty sure I can train him to run with the bike."

They sit in silence.

"Hey, what in the world is with you? You're not usually negative Nancy."

Camas is quiet, not her natural state. "We always do things together. You keep up with me and I keep up with you...well, not quite, but nearly, and we end up together in the end. It's just that lately, since you got master water dog here,

Pedro, and now you're set on this Ironman... woman, idea, well, I'm worried I won't see you."

Tilly hears the voice of her kindergarten best friend in her words.

"That could never happen. If I decide to do this, I'll need your help. I'll need you to be my coach."

"Really?"

"You'd have to chill a bit with the beer offerings. But yes!"

Camas brightens, "Well, of course, silly. I'm the only one who could whip your skinny ass into shape."

"Yes, I know."

"I just remembered something," Camas says excitedly.

"What's that?"

"Liz at the store has an old friend who stopped by to order some things. He asked about you and wanted to apologize."

"Apologize about what?"

"That he was rude to you. Ring a bell?"

Tilly pauses to think. "The old man on the island? That guy didn't seem to be able to do anything but angrily bark."

Pedro barks.

"I trust your astute observation, but Liz told me he wanted to apologize."

"That's surprising."

"This guy on the island, the grumpy old dude, is a major former cycling guy, a real athlete. Or, at least a former athlete. Why don't we ask Liz if he'll train you?"

Camas quickly corrects herself and sits up tall. "Train you in cycling, that is. P will train you in swimming, and I'll train you in running."

"Assuming I would want to have that mean old guy coach me, what makes you think he'd do it?"

"He's up there in his crow's nest in the boondocks not

doing anything else. Why wouldn't he? But mainly, it's just a feeling I have."

"Lucky for you, I believe in that stuff." Tilly smiles, then asks playfully, "What can I do to pay you as my coach? You know I'm poor."

"You can pay me by introducing me as your coach in front of all of the handsome guys caught in your triathlete wake."

"They're all yours!"

"Cheers!" Camas raises her glass to meet Tilly's, "Here's to Tilly, Ironwoman!"

CHAPTER 15
ART DECO 1923 WALNUT BURL
ARMOIRE WITH BAKELITE PULLS

Liz sits at her design desk in a small cabin overlooking the lake and sings along to Madeleine Peyroux's Don't Cry, Baby. She has a desk lamp to illuminate her workspace as she sketches a cycling jersey. She lifts the sketch, picks up some alpaca fabric, holds it to her cheek, and closes her eyes.

She puts the drawing and fabric down and walks to an antique art deco armoire, opens the cabinet door, and pulls out a photo in a frame along with a tiny silver charm in the shape of a castle. She dusts the picture off to reveal a grainy colored image of a young, smiling couple standing with road bikes on a mountainous road in the Italian Alps. The man holds a leather sandal in the air triumphantly.

Liz looks intently at the photo and small charm, starts to put them back in the armoire but pauses and places them on her drawing board instead.

Bear dismounts his horse in front of the cabin, and Frida rushes out to greet him. Bear ties up the horse, then bends over to pick her up and does not put her down. She looks intently at his face and he at hers and they kiss deeply. He puts her down gently.

"It's worse than I thought," he says solemnly.

Liz puts merchandise away in her store as she hums along to the music playing. A young girl at the counter helps a couple with a little boy. She rings up two house-made vegetarian meatloaf sandwiches, chips, two beers, a homemade oatmeal raisin cookie and a carton of chocolate milk.

The wall phone rings and the young girl calls out to Liz, "It's for you."

Liz walks behind the counter and takes the phone, "Hello?"

"Liz, it's Graeme."

"Hi, Graeme. What a nice surprise."

"Do you remember Bill?"

"Yes, of course."

"He's going to come and pick up my things when they arrive."

"It's all here." She feels a bit of disappointment that Graeme will not be returning soon but says perkily, "That's nice of him to pick them up. When's he coming?"

"I was hoping tomorrow and that you'd join us for dinner."

"Hmmm... I think I can," she pauses, considering. "That would be nice to join you all for dinner. Let me see if I can get the store covered. Can I get back to you with an email?"

"I don't have email."

"Well, maybe it's time you turned your computer on," Liz teases.

Graeme laughs. "Maybe I should. Bill will be at the store to pick you up at 5:00 pm tomorrow unless I hear from you."

"I look forward to it. Bye, Graeme."

Liz hangs up the phone. She glances at the young girl, raises her eyebrows and smiles, then looks out over the river, "The hermit can cook it turns out."

Bill drives a vintage convertible through the Okanagan wine country with his wife, Patricia. Patricia is in her sixties with blond-grey hair and looks like an elegant actress straight out of a Golden Era movie in her dark sunglasses and a flamingo-pink silk scarf around her head. Bill's cell phone rings and he answers it on the car's speakerphone.

"Is everything alright?"

"Yes. I'm just calling you," Graeme responds.

"I'm surprised you're calling me. You haven't called me in three years. I thought you didn't have a phone."

"Funny. Remember when you said to ask you if I ever needed anything?"

"Yes, of course."

"Well, I need something. I need you to pick some things up for me at the Herd River Store and bring them to my house."

"Sure, that's no problem. When do you need the stuff?"

"Tomorrow."

"Tomorrow? I'm in Summerland in the Okanagan Valley with Patricia."

"Hi, Patricia. I miss you."

"I miss you too, darling," she shouts over the breezy road noise.

"... And I need you to pick up Liz and bring her too. And also take her back after dinner. Patricia, please come to."

"Graeme, I don't understand the rush. Why..."

Patricia interrupts, "Of course we will. Where do we go, and when?"

"Just search the Herd River Store. It's a local institution. I told Liz to be ready at 5:00 pm."

"What's the cargo weight?"

"Not much. Four or five boxes, including two cases of wine."

"Not a problem."

"I've been training."

"That's excellent news!" Bill exclaims.

"We'll bring dessert," Patricia adds.

CHAPTER 16
RED FLINT AND TINDER 2013 10-YEAR HOODIE WITH CONSPICUOUS STITCHING REPAIR

Tilly, Pedro and Camas run down a pretty country road. They pass an alpaca farm, green alfalfa fields, cottage vegetable gardens, pickup trucks with weathered paint and quaint farmhouses. The smell of old roses fills the air. Camas is sporting a bright red hoodie and blows a whistle in short bursts behind Tilly.

"Will you stop with the bloody whistle already!"

"I'm coaching you."

"You're giving me a headache is what you're doing."

"I'm the old mother in The Triplets of Belleville."

"Sorry, I don't have any idea what you're talking about."

"It's a classic coaching method."

Camas continues to blow the whistle in short bursts behind Tilly. Pedro growls at the whistle and tries to steal it away from Camas.

"Good dog, P."

The girls see Liz riding about a quarter-mile ahead of them on an upright Dutch bike. She hears the whistle and turns around with a curious look, then stops to wait for the girls to catch up.

"Hi, ladies! P! How are you?" Liz reaches down to pet Pedro. "What are you three up to?"

"We're coming to see you. Would you have time to talk with us for a few minutes?"

"Sure. I just need to get the store opened up, and then we can talk."

"Great, thanks!"

Tilly and Camas ride with Liz to her store as Pedro runs along behind. Liz goes into the store, and Tilly and Camas sit outside at a picnic table to wait. Pedro runs off to play in the river.

"You let me do all the talking," Camas says bossily.

"How do you think I would ever get to talk when I'm with you?"

"That's cold."

"It's the truth, but I like that about you," Tilly says with a smile.

Liz comes out with three coffees and two pastries on an antique metal tray. The Herd River Store is an old mercantile known for its delicious homemade foods, baked goods, cheeses, and cured meats from sustainably raised animals as well as its extensive selection of wine and craft beer. Liz sets down the tray and sits down next to Camas.

"Thank you, Liz," Tilly says as she picks up a pastry.

"Oh, no you don't," Camas says as she snags the pastry out of her hand. "Here you go." She hands Tilly a couple of small cycling energy pods.

"Hey, I don't want to eat this astronaut food."

"You're in training, remember?"

Liz looks intrigued. "Training? What are you training for?"

"I've deci..."

Camas cuts her off, "She's doing an Ironman. I'm her coach."

Camas looks very proud.

"Wow, Tilly, that's great. You're such a great athlete."

"I'm not sure about that, but that's why we're here, besides your amazing food... if I could only get a bite," Tilly says as she snatches the pastry back and takes a big bite out of it, glaring at Camas defiantly.

Camas gives her a perturbed look. Tilly waves the back of her hand in the air for Camas to continue talking as she eats.

"Yes, that's right. When I saw you last week, you told me about the man who wanted to apologize to Tilly."

"Yes, that's Graeme. Tilly, he wanted me to pass along his apologies for being so grumpy and inhospitable."

"You also mentioned that he's a former cyclist. Like, a major player in cycling back in the day."

"Yes, he was. He was on the Spericolato team in the 1997 Tour de France. It was an Italian team with a couple of American riders. He got injured and had to leave the team."

"How do you two know each other?" Tilly asks.

"We traveled around Europe for a few years. I cycled too. It was really wonderful, those years."

"Wow, I bet," Tilly says.

"Would he train Tilly?" Camas blurts out. She quickly corrects herself. "Well, I'm the head trainer, so, technically, he would be working under me, but he would be in charge of her cycling training. Tilly doesn't even have a bike yet, and she needs to get up to speed and fast, no pun intended, if she's going to do this Ironman thing."

"Well, I'm not sure," Liz says, surprised. "He's become somewhat of a recluse. Not somewhat. A real hermit. You saw how he acted when you met him."

Tilly nods.

Tilly and Camas look hopefully at Liz. Seeing them with such unbridled optimism brings back memories of herself at their age and she quickly turns upbeat, "But, I can certainly ask him. I'm seeing him tonight, actually. I'll ask him!"

"Thank you, Liz. We appreciate it," Tilly says.

"Can I have another one of those pastries, please?"

"You don't need another pastry, Cam."

"The hell I don't. This coaching gig is burning a lot of calories."

"Of course, Camas," Liz says, laughing. "I'll be right back with one."

Tilly starts to get money out of her backpack.

"No, no, it's on me," Liz insists.

"Thanks again, Liz. P, let's go!" Tilly calls to Pedro down at the shore.

Camas takes several hurried bites of the pastry as Pedro races out of the river and shakes off near the girls. Tilly and Camas hug Liz goodbye and take off running down the road. Camas uses the whistle, and Tilly flashes her a dirty look. Pedro tries to get the whistle out of her hand again and then barks twice at Tilly. Tilly takes off in a sprint.

"Barking works better than my whistle?" Camas shouts behind them, trying to catch up, "Hey, you'll peak too soon! Slow down!"

Liz laughs as she goes back into the store, hearing rhythmic whistle bursts interspersed with Pedro's barks.

CHAPTER 17

WALNUT AND BRASS 1959 MID-CENTURY TERRACE BAR CART

Bill's float plane lands on the river in front of the Herd River Store at exactly 4:49 p.m. Liz comes out to greet him in a pair of jeans and a white blouse, a small scarf around her neck and rope-wedge shoes with painted opalescent "bubble bath" pink, jewel-like toenails. "A pretty toenail makes the woman," her mother used to say.

Liz waves from the porch, and Bill steps out of the plane to greet her. They meet each other on the lawn. He gives her a kiss on both cheeks, and she reciprocates with a strong hug.

"You look fabulous, Liz. It's been too long. Patricia is on the plane. She's dying to see you."

Liz waives at Patricia and blows a kiss.

"Where are the things that need to go to Graeme?"

"Just there, on the porch," she points.

"Jimmy, will you please load those things."

"Nice landing," Liz says to the pilot.

"Thanks," Jimmy says with a proud smile.

They load up. Liz kisses Patricia went she gets on the plane and Jimmy starts the propellor. With their headsets on, the plane pulls away from the dock and begins to gather speed quickly on its pontoons along the still surface of the narrow river, then lifts off. From the sky, they see the winding Lewis Fork River empty out into the vast lake. Some small islands can be seen below with a few motorboats and sailboats. The steep glacier-formed mountains frame their view.

Graeme nervously adjusts his shirt and runs his fingers through his hair in the bedroom mirror as Roxie sits at his feet, looking up at her handsome master adoringly.

"I think this is about as good as it's going to get, Rox."

Roxie kisses his hand and rubs against his leg.

"Thanks, girl."

Patricia, Liz and Bill talk happily over the plane headsets, catching up on each other's lives. Jimmy tries to interject a witty comment here and there, or an observation about what they are passing over. After fifteen minutes in the air, the seaplane touches down on the lake and taxies to Graeme's dock.

"That is always so much fun. The lake landing!" Liz laughs.

"I never tire of it either!" Patrica agrees.

Ike and Suerte are soundly asleep on the deck of the boat and wake up with a start when Ike's flip phone rings in his pocket. Ike fumbles to find his phone, and opens it as Suerte jumps off his lap, startled, then runs into the cabin.

"Ouch, Suert! Yeah?"

"Ike, it's Bear. You OK?"

"Yep, just some cat claws in my leg. No permanent damage. Just a little blood."

"We need to talk."

"Sure, buddy."

"I rode up to Blue Lightning, and Tilly was right. They're logging just above the Kootenai sacred. Not only that, they're loggin' a piece that's very steep and unstable. I think they somehow snuck that by the Idaho Department of Lands. I'm worried about the sacred grounds and also the town. It looks way too much like the ground above Oso."

"Oso?"

"Don't you remember? The logging mudslide in '94 that slid over 300 acres and killed thirty people."

"Shit."

"I know the mayor. He's a young guy, just getting his paws wet but a good man. I'll see if he has any pull."

"Let him know the urgency. Those bureaucrats are so damn slow."

"Will do," Bear says solemnly.

Roxie rushes down to greet the plane. Bill and Patricia arrive at the top of the trail and meet Graeme with hugs. Graeme kisses Patricia on both cheeks warmly as he looks distractedly beyond her in search of Liz.

Patricia notices and whispers, "She's right behind us."

Roxie races around the last turn and pops out at the top of the trail. Liz follows close behind, walking gracefully up the path with a warm smile.

"So this is where you've been holed up all of these months. It's lovely."

"Thank you. You're lovely," Graeme says, taking her hand.

Liz smiles. "We have your supplies on the plane."

Bill overhears. "Don't worry about that. I asked Jimmy to bring everything up."

"Thanks, Bill," Graeme and Liz say in unison. They smile, a bit embarrassed, realizing that a past life is resurfacing.

The guests walk to Graeme's patio and pour themselves a drink from a small mid-century bar cart outside. Liz pours Patricia a glass of Columbia River Sauvignon Blanc, then one for herself. Bill makes himself a Scotch and water. They talk and laugh as they mingle, looking out over the beautiful lake with the reflections of the warm colors of the sunset dancing across it. Things get quiet for a few minutes.

"I'm going to go check on Jimmy," Liz announces abruptly.

"No, Liz, he's fine. He'll be right up."

"It's OK. There were a lot of things." She rushes away, "I'll be right back." Bill shrugs helplessly and sits down on a patio chair. Patricia leans over and kisses him. "I'm going to check on Graeme," she says as she walks inside.

Bill pets Roxie. "Looks like it's just you and me, girl."

Roxie follows Patricia inside. Bill shrugs.

"This looks beautiful, Graeme. Can I help you?" Patricia asks.

"I think I have it covered. I used to know how to do this. I'm not sure now, but we'll see what we get."

"Liz went down to check on the things you ordered."

The two are quiet for a couple of minutes as Patricia watches Graeme put the fish filets on a platter and season them. She sips her wine. Finally, she breaks the silence.

"Wow, Graeme. You and Liz, here together. It's really nice."

Graeme kisses her on the cheek. "Thanks, Patricia. I hope it's nice for everyone."

Liz and Jimmy walk up from a road behind the cottage,

each pushing handcarts, Jimmy with four boxes, Liz with two. Graeme sees them, opens the back screen door, and rushes to grab the cart from Liz. Jimmy stops outside with his cart to answer a phone call.

"Oh, Liz, I'm sorry. You shouldn't have had to get that."

"It's fine. Now we don't have to bother with it later. What you're doing is much more important. Smells great!"

"Thanks."

"Your jersey is in there too. If you decide it's not right, I'll take it back. No problem."

"Kids, I'm going back out with Bill. Let me know if you need anything," Patricia says, as she leaves the kitchen.

"I know I'll like it. Thank you so much and for all of the other things from the store too."

"Can I help you with dinner?"

"You can help me keep Roxie from trying to eat our dinner!"

Liz laughs and mock-scolds Roxie as she pets her, "You should know better."

Graeme and Liz smile at each other and stand very close. They start to lean in slightly, possibly for a kiss and are interrupted by Jimmy.

"Hey, where can a thirsty pilot get a beer?"

"There are plenty in the refrigerator. Help yourself."

Jimmy grabs a beer and heads towards the patio. "Thanks, man."

"You invited that guy to dinner?" Graeme asks with a wince.

"It seemed so cold to leave him waiting on the plane."

"It was a sweet gesture." Graeme adds skeptically, "I'll have Roxie keep an eye on him."

CHAPTER 18

BARRISTER WINERY 2008
CABERNET FRANC

The sun is low in the sky, and the golden glow shines on the lake below as the five sit for dinner on Graeme's patio. Graeme has picked some Miles Davis, and the bright jazz notes bounce around the table perfectly complementing the freshly caught fish, ripe fruit of the wine, and abundant laughter.

Jimmy is loud, commandeering much of the conversation. "Did you hear the one about the blonde and the pilot who dies in the cockpit?"

"No, Jimmy, I don't believe we have," Bill responds good-humoredly.

Graeme rolls his eyes. He turns to Liz to talk as Jimmy tells a joke in the background.

"The pilot has a heart attack and dies. The blonde, frantic, calls out..."

"This is lovely wine. What is it?" Liz asks Graeme.

Jimmy continues his joke in falsetto, *"May Day! May Day! Help me! Help me! My pilot had a heart attack and is dead, and I don't know how to fly. Help me! Please help me!"*

"It's a 2008 Barrister Cab Franc."

"She hears a voice over the radio saying…" Jimmy continues in a low, official-sounded voice, *This is Air Traffic Control, and I hear you loud and clear. I'll talk you through this and get you back on the ground. Now, just take a deep breath. Everything will be fine! Now give me your height and position."*

Liz and Graeme stop for a moment to hear the punch line.

Jimmy looks to see if everyone is listening. Pleased that they are, he finishes, "And the blonde says," again in falsetto, *I'm five foot four inches, and I'm in the front seat."* He bursts out laughing at his joke.

Graeme grimaces as the rest of the group laugh dutifully.

Liz turns back to Graeme, "Remember the girl you asked me to apologize to on your behalf, for being so grumpy?"

Bill butts in, "What? Graeme needing to apologize for being grumpy? Unheard of."

Patricia puts her hand on Bill's leg and shakes her head.

"Yes, I remember."

"Her name is Tilly, and her best friend is Camas. Tilly has decided to do an Ironman."

"That girl can swim," Graeme says.

"She's been swimming this lake all her life. She's also a long-distance runner. Have you seen her run?"

"I doubt it since he's a recluse on an island," Bill blurts out again.

"Bill," Patricia scolds.

"She and Camas are both impressive runners. They came to see me this morning. Ran to see me, to see if I would ask you a question."

"What question?"

"If you would train Tilly in cycling."

Graeme has a confused look. "That's crazy," Graeme says, surprised.

"Why is it crazy?" Liz asks gently.

"Why would I train her?"

"Why wouldn't you?" Bill asks.

Everyone leans in to listen.

"I'm just relaying their request," Liz says sweetly, seeing Graeme's discomfort with the question.

"Somehow, they found out about my past." He looks pointedly at her.

"I was telling Camas about a bike jersey I was making, and she asked how I got the idea. You know, your background is quite public if someone wanted to learn about you."

"I know." Graeme looks away.

"I hope you'll think it over."

"Tell her I can't," he says firmly.

"Really? You're not even going to consider it?!"

"No."

"What are you doing that would prevent you from helping her?"

Bill, Patricia and Jimmy look at each other helplessly.

"Even if I did have time, why would I?"

Bill interjects, "Because you can? Because you just started training, and maybe there's a reason for that. Because maybe this is the next phase of your career? It sounds perfect for you."

"Perfect? ...Perfect?!" Graeme's voice rises into a loud timbre. "How could training a woman who has never even cycled before be perfect? Sounds like a disaster!"

Liz stands up abruptly, bumps the table, and knocks her wine glass over. Flustered by Graeme's outburst and the red wine spill, she picks up her purse and steps away from the table.

"Well, I was wrong about you, I see. I thought for certain you'd evolved during all this time on the island. Seems you're just as stubborn, self-centered, and neanderthal as before. Thank you for dinner." She turns to Bill and Patricia, "I'm sorry. I'll be on the plane but please don't rush. Take your time."

Liz walks away towards the path down to the dock. Under her breath, she says, "Stubborn ass."

Liz sits on the plane, looking out the window toward the lake. The sun touches the horizon. Jimmy stands by the plane door waiting for Patricia and Bill, who are on the dock talking to Graeme.

"What in the world happened? Things were going so well," Patricia says, holding Graeme's forearms.

"You tell me."

"Promise me you'll give Liz's request some thought. She's a wise woman. It would be good for you," Bill says in the best listen-to-your-uncle voice he could muster.

"Travel safely," Graeme says, with a serious expression as he kisses Patricia on the cheek and shakes Bill's hand firmly.

Bill and Patricia get back on the plane. Jimmy unties the boat from the dock and hops into the pilot's seat. Liz turns to look back at the island. Graeme waves and Roxie barks. Without a smile, Liz quickly turns her head back around. The plane lifts off over the lake into the setting sun.

"That's a nice view, but why would anyone want to live out there all by themselves?" Jimmy says over the plane headsets.

"Shush, Jimmy," Patricia gives Jimmy a serious look.

"It's OK, Patricia," Liz says, looking out the window.

"Graeme has some demons. If you ask me, he's finally coming out of his cave, out of that prison he created in his mind," Bill says.

"I was hoping so."

"Sometimes, that doesn't happen overnight. I think he's creeping out. Not leaping out," Bill adds.

"I saw glimmers. I miss him."

Patricia reaches over to hold Liz's hand. "I can tell he misses you too."

The airplane engine sings a melancholy tune home and lands safely down on the river with its passengers, as a beautiful golden sunset sky fades behind it. They all exit the plane. Standing on the dock, Bill and Patricia hug Liz. Jimmy walks over and kisses her on the cheek.

"Thank you, all."

Liz walks towards the store and turns to wave to them as they fly off.

CHAPTER 19

HENRY HUGHES & SON LTD. 1850
BRASS AND MAHOGANY OFFICER
OF WATCH TELESCOPE

Tilly drives along the winding lakeside road and talks to Camas on her cell phone speaker.

"I just got off work," Camas said.

"P and I are headed to the marina to swim."

"Nice. How far?"

"Not sure, coach."

"How about to Opal Island and back?"

"Did you hear what he said?"

"That's why I'm calling. He said no."

Tilly is silent.

Camas breaks the silence, "I'm sorry Till. We don't need the geezer."

"That sucks. Did he say why?"

"No. Just something along the lines of, 'why would I?'... like he's too good for it or something."

Tilly is silent. She hears her phone beep, glances at it. "Gotta go, Cam. Ike is calling."

"OK, be safe. Swim like a dolphin, iron princess."

Tilly taps her cell phone. "Hi, Ike... so your phone works!"

"Will you be near the marina anytime soon?"

"P and I are headed your way now to swim."

"Stop by. I need to tell you something."

"Can you tell me now?"

"I hate these god damn phones. Just stop by, please."

"No problem. See you in five."

Pedro's head hangs out of the truck window as they drive along the coast. Tilly sees Opal Island in the distance and shakes her head. She feels a mixture of confusion and frustration bubbling up inside her.

They arrive at the marina, and Tilly carries her paddleboard along the dock, then puts the board in the water near Ike's boat.

"P, lie down. Stay."

Pedro barks. Suerte, asleep on the top of the boat, wakes with a start, jumps up, and accidentally falls into the water.

"Ike, cat overboard!"

Ike rushes out of the cabin. "Damn cat!"

He scoops Suerte out of the water with the net. The cat snarls at Pedro, then sulks away, dripping wet.

"I'm not sure if that's a cat or a dog," Ike says.

Tilly smiles. "No wonder I like Suerte so much. Did you hear from Bear?"

"Sit down."

Tilly sits down on a bench on the boat deck.

"Bear found the logging operation you saw. They're about an eighth of a mile above the Kootenai sacred grounds."

"Shit."

"Yes, major shit. What's more, they're logging a very steep piece of ground. Bear said he confronted the foreman. He's got some history with the guy, total city slicker asshole, and the son of a bitch couldn't produce the permit."

"Shit."

"Bear says the site is very similar in slope and topography to the one that caused that slide in Oso."

"Really? I remember that. It was a big disaster."

"Yup. Bear's going over to see the mayor today. If it slides, that debris will affect the town's water supply at best. At worst, it could hit some homes."

"I know Pat, the mayor too. I'll check in with him. Can't hurt."

"Bear said they hadn't started the steepest part yet, but we don't have much time."

"Thanks, Ike," Tilly says weakly.

Tilly steps off the boat onto the paddleboard with Pedro.

"Let's go, P."

Tilly paddles out of the marina onto the open lake. Pedro begins to pace back and forth.

"Sorry, P. I'm first today."

Tilly takes her board shorts and T-shirt off and wears a surfer-girl two-piece. Her body is tense, nothing like her flowing yoga form, and her head hangs low. She dives in, circles back and ties the harness around her hips, then swims to the board and kisses Pedro with a forlorn look.

"What is this world coming to, P? Lie down. Stay."

Pedro whimpers and lies down at the front of the board.

Tilly swims slowly at first and then increases her speed to a vigorous, steady pace.

Graeme sits at his desk at the window overlooking the lake. Roxie comes up to him with a cycling shoe.

"No, girl. Not today."

She brings the other shoe and bumps his leg with it.

"No, Roxie. Stop," with a louder voice.

Roxie pushes the box that Liz brought from the kitchen into the living room. She pushes and pushes until it is at Graeme's feet.

"Damn dog. I love you."

Graeme pats her gently as he walks out to the trainer frame. He raises his captain's telescope to his eye to see Tilly swimming fast. A boat travels on the other side of her in the same direction. The distance creates the illusion they are racing.

"That girl is strong, Rox."

Tilly begins to swim harder and faster. Pedro stands up, concerned, and starts to pace. Tilly increases her intensity and speed. From Graeme's vista, the speed boat seems to be on a path that will intersect Tilly's. Pedro barks loud, repeated warnings, but Tilly doesn't stop swimming. She keeps up her fast pace.

Pedro backs up a couple of steps and then runs and leaps off the front of the board. The speed boat races closer. Pedro swims fast towards Tilly. The speed boat's passengers are laughing and distracted, beer cozies in their hands, their watercraft a bullet on the lake.

Pedro swims faster, his panting breath not heard above the boat's engine. His legs, made strong from miles of swimming with Tilly, and his water dog webbed paws give him the extra propulsion needed to catch her. He snatches the small floating ball on the harness in his teeth. Tilly feels it, shrugs slightly, and keeps swimming. Pedro tugs, holds firm, then makes a strong deliberate turn to swim in the opposite direction, his water dog fisherman genes holding him in good stead. Perhaps his DNA remembers dragging those heavy Portuguese fishing nets? Tilly swerves from Pedro's counter tug and looks up just as the speed boat notices the two of them and swerves.

"What the Hemlock!" the boat driver shouts.

Tilly gasps for breath from the crashing realization of the near-miss. She and Pedro swim to the board. She climbs up, pulls him up to her, and sobs into his neck.

"I'm so sorry, P," she cries.

Pedro licks her face and tears gently.

At a distance, the boat makes a circle around the paddle-board. The driver calls, "Are you OK?!"

Tilly gives the boat a weak thumbs up.

"So, you think maybe you should take the reigns?"

Pedro licks her again.

"OK, handsome. P, swim!" Tilly says, raising her arm to motion Pedro to dive in.

Pedro jumps in and brings Tilly the harness in his mouth. She fastens it to him, and he happily pulls the paddleboard, one paw in front of the other again and again.

Tilly rests on the board, lying on her stomach. She looks ahead for a little bit, scanning the horizon for more boats, then lays her head down on her arms in a state of melancholy, an emotion not familiar to her in many years. She is gradually comforted by the sounds of Pedro panting and swimming.

"That doesn't look like training for an Ironman race to me," a male voice calls from behind.

Startled, Tilly sits up quickly. Graeme and Roxie are a few boat lengths behind in a kayak.

"What are you doing here?" Tilly asks as she wipes tears from her eyes.

"I live here."

"You live in the lake?"

"You know where I live."

"Yes, I do."

Pedro slows down when he sees the boat.

"P, stop. Come!" Tilly calls.

Pedro swims back to the board. He is very excited to see Roxie and doggie-paddles right past the paddleboard to the kayak, turning the board to face Graeme.

"P, come."

Pedro ignores her command.

Graeme lifts Pedro into the kayak, and the two dogs kiss each other. Graeme unties his harness.

"Looks like they missed each other," Graeme says, smiling at the dogs.

"What are you doing here?" Tilly asks seriously.

"I heard you want to do an Ironman race."

"That's right."

"I clocked you swimming. You were swimming better than an Ironman pace for over thirty minutes."

"I was upset."

"Upset about what?" Graeme asks.

"Couple of things."

"Like what?"

"I heard you weren't interested in helping me learn to cycle."

"Well, I'm a selfish old bastard."

"That sucks if it's true."

"I'm trying to soften up. What's the other thing?"

"There's a logging company about to pile a million logs on top of my ancestors' sacred grounds."

"Over off Blue Lightning?"

"You know it?"

"I used to visit it when I was out cycling and needed to think. So, why are you out swimming in the middle of a huge lake when you should be stopping those bastards?"

Tilly looks helpless. She throws her hands up towards the sky, as if looking for help.

"First lesson of your cycling training," Graeme says

69

intently. "... The gods help those who help themselves. The universe honors us when we show our best effort."

Tilly looks surprised. She was silent, then asks, "You are training me?"

"Repeat lesson one, please."

"The gods help those who help themselves." She pauses to think. "... The universe honors us when we show our best effort."

Graeme nods. Pedro and Roxie seem to nod as well.

"Now what?" Tilly asks.

"Let's go to town and see the mayor," Graeme says, as he takes hold of his paddle. "Follow me to my dock, and I'll get the boat."

Graeme paddles with the dogs as Tilly follows on her board. They pull the kayak onto the dock, hoist the paddleboard into Graeme's vintage boat, and head across the lake to Sandglass.

CHAPTER 20
BULLDOG WIGAN ENGLAND 1919
GARDEN HAND TROWEL

Liz says hello to the happy people picnicking on the store's outdoor tables in the warm afternoon sun as she walks to the dock. She wears a tank top, long mountain biking shorts and a backpack. She loads a mountain bike into the front of a small motorboat, starts it up and heads down the river. Twenty minutes later, she arrives at the small dock at the trailhead to Bear and Frida's cabin.

Liz bikes up the trail. Her graceful flow is in stark contrast to Ike's wild style. She has a serious expression as she emerges from the tall trees onto the pathway leading to the cabin. Bear sees her first and greets her with an Idaho-sky smile.

"Look at the angel floating in."

"Hi Bear!" she says as she gives him a hug, her head reaching his lower chest.

"How are you, Liz?"

"I'm great, thank you. Well, not great actually, but darn good."

"We're on a journey that doesn't ever promise great, but it does promise getting closer to the truth."

"I know," she says and smiles. "Speaking of journey, I'm looking for Frida."

"Frida's at the sacred grounds."

"OK, great, I'll head over there if you don't think she'll mind the company?"

"She'll be so happy to have your company. Be careful, though. There's logging going on nearby. That's why she headed over there. To do some praying with the ancestors."

"OK. Thanks, Bear. I'll be careful."

"Maybe you can join us for supper on your way back?"

"That sounds nice."

Liz gets back on her bike. The wooded trail grows more dense and beautiful with occasional striking lookouts towering over the sparkling lake and meadows of tall bear-grass that look like something straight out of Avatar. Liz exits the trail and finds herself in the clearing of the sacred grounds. Frida kneels, busily planting, working the soil with a small hand trowel. Liz wonders if she may also be praying because her eyes are nearly closed.

Liz leans her bike against a tree and approaches Frida. Frida looks up and smiles. They embrace wordlessly. Frida takes her by the hand, and they walk to sit, side by side atop a knoll with wildflowers surrounding them and sunlight streaming through the tall fir and tamarack trees bordering the clearing. Frida begins to chant. Liz hums beneath the chanting. It is a sweet harmony of old and new as the quaking aspen leaves rustle above them.

Frida stops and turns toward Liz. "I know you're troubled, dear friend."

"More like frustrated. I know I can't control him."

"Would you want to?"

"No."

"You know what to do. You are very strong, Elizabeth of the River."

They move to face each other, still seated on the earth. Frida reaches out to hold both of Liz's hands. They close their eyes.

"We pray for the earth. We pray that we can be wise to know our place among all things, not just humans. We pray to protect these sacred grounds of our ancestors. Do you have an intention you would like the ancestors to hear?" Frida asked.

"May we heal old wounds so we can help others."

"Yes. And so it is."

"And so it is."

They open their eyes and smile at each other as a hawk calls to her mate flying high overhead.

CHAPTER 21
MID-CENTURY MODERN 1962
STEELCASE TANKER DESK

Graeme, Tilly and the dogs step out of the boat onto the Sandglass marina dock. Roxie and Pedro stay close to each other, walking side by side on their leashes. They cross the street to City Hall, a regal brick structure, built in 1909.

"Sorry, no dogs," a security guard says abruptly as they attempt to enter the building.

They step back outside and see two boys playing across the street.

"Hey guys, I'll pay you five bucks each to play with our dogs for about twenty minutes," Graeme hollers.

"Sure!"

Graeme and Tilly enter the building again.

"We're here to see the mayor."

"He's at lunch," the guard says.

"We'll wait, thanks," Tilly responds politely.

"We have some time to kill. Let's sit over here and talk about your training," Graeme says as he walks to a bench outside the mayor's office.

"OK."

"First of all, you should know that all the coaching experience I have is from coaching I've received, not given."

"OK."

"Second, I'll have some opinions and resources for your swimming and running, but I don't know much about that from a technical standpoint."

"Got it."

"Lastly, I'd like to know the reason you want to do this. It may help me help you."

"Alright," Tilly nodded.

Graeme pauses. "Would you like to tell me now?"

"No, not now."

"OK."

"But I do need to tell you something important."

"I'm listening."

"I have a head coach. You'll be reporting to her."

Graeme raises his eyebrows, surprised. "You do, do you? Liz made it sound as though you were on your own. Sounds like you don't really need me." Graeme looks disappointed.

"You can't work with someone else?"

"I'm a bit of a hard-headed loner."

"Her name's Camas, and she's easy to get along with, especially if you like beer, tequila and whistles."

"Well, I like beer and tequila. But whistles?"

"She's my best friend. She's more of an agent than a head trainer because she's always looking out for my best interests. She's been with me forever, and she can run."

"Hmmm...."

"All I ask is that you're respectful of her ideas." Tilly pauses. "... It would also be quite helpful if you were a tad deferential."

"Deferential, huh? I'll try to manage that."

"Thank you."

"So, what do you know about the Ironman?" Graeme asks.

"I know it is 2.4 miles of swimming, 112 miles of cycling and a 26-mile run."

"Anything else?"

"I know there's a series of competitions across the planet, and that only the top athletes qualify to compete in Kona."

"Is your goal Kona?"

"My goal's to swim my best and improve in the other sports. I don't think I have to do that in Kona."

"Good. Nice kids like you can get burned out or worse yet, hurt, with unrealistic goals."

"You don't think I can get to Kona?" Tilly says proudly.

"I like that you want to do your best. Let's just leave it at that."

Tilly feels perturbed at what seems to be doubts about her abilities. After a pause, she says, "You should know that I don't have money to pay you or to buy a bike."

The handsome, thirty-year-old mayor, wearing jeans with a tweed blazer over a polo shirt, walks through the door with a quick step, interrupting them.

"Tilly! How are you?" the mayor says, as he kisses her on the cheek. "And Graeme! You're on the mainland! So nice to see you both!"

"Mayor, we need your help," Graeme says.

"Sure. Come, sit," he says warmly, as he motions them into the office.

Tilly and Graeme sit down in front of the mayor's desk.

"What's up?"

"Why don't you tell the mayor, Tilly."

"Sure. Patrick... I mean mayor, there's logging going on just above the Kootenai sacred grounds, off of Blue Lightning road. Bear visited, and they're soon going to be logging an extremely steep hill that could slide."

"Bear came to see me about this too."

"It's serious," Tilly adds, in a passionate tone.

"Mayor, if there's a slide, part of the town is right in its path," Graeme adds.

"After we're done here, I'll call the logging company to get to the bottom of this."

"Can you issue an order for them to stop, at least until they produce the permit?"

"I would need to get a judge to do that, but if I don't have it by five tonight, I'll call Judge Clark first thing in the morning."

"Thanks, Pat," Graeme says.

"You're welcome."

The mayor shakes hands with Graeme and gives Tilly another kiss on the cheek goodbye. They walk out and cross the street to pay the boys and retrieve the dogs.

"Thanks for that, Graeme," Tilly says as they walk back to the marina. "When do we start cycling?"

"Let's meet on Saturday. I'll get to work on finding you a bike."

"OK, where should I meet you?"

"Meet me at Sylvester Bay at eight a.m. There's a large grassy area near the main parking lot at the boat launch."

"OK."

"Can you get home from here? I'll take your board to the marina for you."

"Sure."

Graeme leans down and speaks quietly to Pedro as he pets him, "I saw that near-miss with the boat today. Good dog."

Graeme calls, "Let's go, Rox."

Roxie reluctantly walks away with Graeme, looking back at Pedro. Tilly smiles.

"Hey, what's going on up at Blue Lightening? I've had two visits today from citizens telling me you're logging a site that should be off-limits," the mayor says firmly into his cell phone. He listens.

"What do you mean, never mind? They say that your logging mess is going to end up on top of the city," he continues, raising his voice.

He speaks louder, his face reddening, "Email me the permit by five pm tonight or I'll ask Judge Clark to shut you down tomorrow. No later than five!"

He ends the call angrily, and his phone drops onto his mid-century metal desk with a loud bang. He picks it up, stuffs it into his backpack, then grabs his bike that is resting against the wall. He walks out, slamming the door behind him.

Gary drives a large pick-up truck on Blue Lightning Road. His son Dust, a young man in his twenties with brown hair in a buzz-cut, wearing a logger helmet with screen mesh face cover and ear muffs and a T-shirt that reads *Trees Make Big Houses* under his long-sleeve flannel shirt, sits in the passenger seat. Gary picks up his phone as the truck maneuvers the bumpy, rutted road.

"Judge, we'll have your logs to your home site by tomorrow."

CHAPTER 22

BLUE AND WHITE 1954 15-FOOT FOLBOT CAREFREE TRAVEL CRAFT KAYAK

Tilly walks from the marina to Heaven's Brothers coffee shop. Her excitement about learning to cycle helps soften her worries about the logging activity a bit. She enters the café and sees Camas reading quietly with a cup of tea.

"My my, this is a first. I just went into the Five Nineteen, expecting to see you winning a game of pool, but here you are reading at four in the afternoon with a cup of tea!"

"Did you know that Paula Newby-Fraser won the Ironman World Championship in Hawaii eight times from 1986 to 1996 and was known as the Queen of Kona?"

"Really? No, I didn't."

"Do you want to go to Kona?"

"Cam, I don't know anything about any of that yet. There's a slight chance I might be up to the challenge in swimming because I did pretty well in some high school races... but I don't even know if I'm fast enough in that sport, let alone the running, or the cycling. I have something to tell you."

Camas continues reading her book.

"Cam, I'm trying to tell you something important."

"Sorry. Shoot."

"I met the old cycling dude out on the lake today. I was swimming this morning, and he came up to me in his old school kayak. He's going to coach me."

"Really! That's awesome!" She turns concerned, "You told him I'm your head coach though, right?"

"Of course. You're in charge. He admits that he's not very up on swimming or running."

"When do we start?"

"Eight am Saturday, at Sylvester Bay," Tilly answers excitedly.

"That's kind of a weird spot. And early."

"Yep."

"If this guy's nuts, we can fire him."

"I think he might be nuts, but in a good way. Kind of like your brand of nuts," Tilly said with a smile.

"Hey!" Camas laughed.

"I'm running to the marina to get my truck."

"Do you want a ride?"

"I need the run. P already had a long swim. Can you drop him at my house?"

"Sure," Camas says as she leans down pet him.

"I'm off," Tilly says, as she runs out the door.

"Be safe!" Camas calls out.

"Come on, handsome. Let's go get a beer before we go home. Boys like girls with a dog. You can be my wingman."

Tilly runs through the wooded trails along the lake with the water glowing under the late afternoon sun. She listens to a contemporary folk song with her headphones in one ear as she runs. She hums at first, then sings the words out loud, as her breath falls in time with her steps and the rhythm of her pace. She runs at a good clip, which requires agility as the trail twists and turns with many stones. Her light singing turns into her full voice as she arrives at an overlook. She stops, looks out over the water, still sweetly singing the song. The words of the song meld into a Native American chant. She closes her eyes, and her body sways with the breeze and the music, and she lifts her arms to the sky.

"Thank you," she says as she looks upwards.

Tilly arrives at Ike's boat and gives a loud shout, "Ike!"

Ike is sound asleep, sunken into his chair, surrounded by books on the deck. He wakes, startled. Suerte, sleeping nearby, jumps into the air and runs into the cabin out of sight.

"Tilly!" he says happily.

"I want to thank you for going to see Bear. He went to see Mayor Pat, and I did too. We'll know more tomorrow morning. Sorry to wake you so suddenly."

"No, no. Don't be sorry. I'm so happy to get the update."

"Ike, this isn't over yet. We may need your help again."

"You know I'm a solitary guy and generally keep to myself, but I don't have a pirate's flag for nothin'. You just let me know if you need help."

"I will. Thanks, Ike."

"It's been a long day. I'm getting my truck and heading home to get P and to sleep."

"Sleep well, princess T."

They hug, and Tilly runs to her truck as Ike watches her protectively from the boat. Suerte jumps back into Ike's lap and purrs.

Tilly arrives home. Her tiny cottage sits on a hill with views of both the town and the lake. Her belongings are well-organized and her house clean, except for some stray dog toys. She throws her keys into a bowl on the counter and calls for Pedro in the back yard. He doesn't come. She walks back onto the front deck overlooking the lights of the small town as she dials Camas.

"Where's my baby?"

"He's here."

"Time to come home, coach. It's nine."

"Nine is early."

"Not for a dog and not for a coach."

"Really?"

"Really."

"OK, let me unwrap the gorgeous eligible Idaho bachelors from me, and we'll head home," she says, sitting alone, not a man from any state in the lower forty-eight or Alaska or Hawaii in sight.

"Now, please."

Tilly waits for Pedro as she listens to music on the deck. Camas pulls up, honks, waves, and then opens the door for Pedro. He bounds up the steps of the porch to Tilly.

Tilly waves and shouts, "Thanks! See you tomorrow morning."

Tilly texts, *Sylvester Bay tomorrow 8am. Set your alarm.*

Camas texts back, *Got it. <3.*

The sun rises over Lake Bijou Nez as Mayor Patrick walks to Heaven's Brothers for his morning coffee. He says hello to the people there before he walks back to his office.

He sits down at his chair, opens his laptop, scrolls for a few seconds, and shakes his head in frustration. He walks over to the fax machine. Nothing. He looks at his phone again for messages.

"Damn."

He dials. "Hello, your honor. How are you today? I'm calling to request an urgent meeting with you for an injunction."

Patrick listens.

"Oh, I'm sorry. I wouldn't ask if it wasn't critical. I've never asked before."

Patrick listens.

"No, sir, tomorrow morning will be too late. I'm so sorry that you have a tee time at Bijou Nez Resort. I know how expensive that is. I can drive to you if need be."

Patrick grimaces.

"No, sir, the ramifications of waiting are potentially a landslide similar to that which took place in Oso a few years ago. There's also a Native American sacred area that may be affected."

He sighs heavily.

"No, sir, that's not the only consideration. The grade of the site is too steep and historically unstable. If it slides, it'll come down on about thirty-five homes."

Patrick listens.

"No, we don't have a report."

Extremely frustrated, running out of steam, his speech slows, "You can't stop it now... because of your tee time?"

The line is silent.

"Judge Clark? Judge? Hello? Hello?"

Patrick slams his fist down on the desk.

CHAPTER 23

UPCYCLED SUITCASE 2010
THUMPCASE RENEGADE ONE
MOBILE PARTY BLUETOOTH
BOOMBOX

Tilly, Camas and Pedro pull into the Sylvester Bay parking lot in Tilly's truck. There is a grassy park overlooking the sparkling lake. In the distance, two pickup trucks idle near the boat ramp, waiting to lower their boats into the water to fish.

The Bike Guys all have well-kept Northern Idaho beards, except for Reeve, who is clean-shaven. Clad in their mountain bike shorts and full of healthy athleticism, they stand next to Graeme and a van parked near the grass. Josh is black, late-twenties, and wears a Greta Thunberg *there is no planet B* T-shirt. Cutter, the tallest of the group at 6'2", wears a beanie over his bright red hair. Joe, in his early twenties, has dark wavy hair and wears jeans with a hoody sweatshirt. Years of water and mountain outdoor adventures forged their bond.

"Good morning," Graeme says as he extends his hand. "You must be Camas. Nice to meet you."

Camas grabs Graeme's hand and shakes it in an awkward business-like fashion.

"These are my good friends, Reeve, Josh, Cutter and Joe."

"We know these guys," Camas laughs as she punches Josh in the arm.

"Ow!" Josh laughs and pretends to be hurt.

"Oh, good. Guys, get the bikes out of the van. Reeve, hang out here with us please."

Graeme leads them to a picnic table and sits down, motioning for the others to sit.

"I want to set..." Graeme stops himself, then looks at Camas, "propose... some ground rules for training if that's OK."

Tilly and Camas nod.

"This is your training, Tilly."

"Whose else would it be?" Camas asks with a sarcastic tone.

Tilly shakes her head at Camas.

"I mean that you'll improve based on your perceived effort. That's how it works. That effort will decrease naturally as you get stronger. I'll propose a framework for your training, and it'll include intense periods, and it will also include rest. Sometimes the rest isn't as easy as it sounds, though, because you may become caught up in the feeling of improving and thinking that by doing more, you'll be improving more. It doesn't work that way."

The girls look curious. Reeve, whose T-shirt reads *mountain biking is not a crime*, a handsome man in his late forties with a face weathered by the sun, nods in agreement and respect.

Graeme continues, "So when we schedule a rest day, that does not mean swimming one mile instead of five, or running ten miles instead of twenty-five. It means rest."

"Rest. OK," Tilly responds.

"Great. One more thing right now. I'll use Brava to track your time and distances, but I don't want you logging into it to compare yourself to other athletes."

"What's Brava?"

"That's good. You won't miss it then. Here's a GPS watch. Reeve will help you figure it out if you need help."

Graeme sees the guys walking up. "Here come the bikes."

Tilly and Camas look up in excitement. Their faces turn to confusion.

"What in the world? Those are funky fixies!" Camas says, her face scrunched.

"Yep."

"What's that on the wheels?"

Each wheel has a cover over its spokes.

"You'll see. Put on the knee pads and gloves, please."

"Tilly has ridden a bike before," Camas says, clearly annoyed.

"Cam," Tilly says firmly, with a do-as-he-asks look.

Reluctantly, Camas puts on the knee pads and gloves and gets on the bike. "This one seems good," she says, resigned.

Reeve walks a bike over to Tilly and she gets on. He adjusts the seat a bit.

She smiles broadly in anticipation. "Ready!"

The group rides over the grass to the tennis court which has the net removed and orange cones marking goals at each end. They all stand circling Graeme with their bikes.

"The bicycle. The greatest invention of all time," Graeme says reverently.

He picks up mallets lying on the court and distributes one to each of them. The girls look surprised. Josh rides to the edge of the court and, without stopping, pushes a button on a custom boom box that has been retrofitted within a vintage suitcase. The upbeat rock music heightens the excitement.

"Bike polo. It's a pretty simple concept. Pass the ball to your teammate. Score a goal and don't be afraid to bump into your competitors a little," Graeme instructs.

"What? Bump into the other bikes? What is this?" Camas questions pointedly.

Tilly whispers, "Cam, shush! You promised."

Graeme continues, "Cycling is about confidence and that means not being afraid of some contact. Camas and Tilly, pick your teams. Camas, you first."

"Reeve," Camas called out.

Tilly follows, "Graeme."

"I'm out because we're only seven."

Graeme looks up, pauses, "Wait, who's that I see?"

They all look up to see Ike riding in on a bike. He takes a spin around the parking lot with the music blaring in the background, then skids up to the group. They laugh.

"Glad you're here, man," Reeve says, giving him a pat on the back.

"I heard there might be a game with some newbies."

Reeve grabs a mallet and wheel covers from the van and hands them to Ike.

"I choose Ike," Camas continues picking teams.

"Joe."

"Cutter," Camas says, smiling at him.

"Josh," Tilly finishes.

"Just like grade school. Always the last one picked."

Pedro who has been following Tilly around, now jumps excitedly, sensing something fun is about to happen. Tilly ties him up on the edge of the court. He whimpers a little, then lies down in resignation.

"OK, Team Tilly: Joe, Josh, me. Captain Camas: Ike, Cutter, Reeve. The basic rules are as follows. If you set a hand or foot on the ground, you're out of play until you ride around and ring the bell at the side of the court. You can shuffle the ball during play but goals can only be scored from a hit using the round end of the mallet."

"Shuffle?" Tilly asks.

"Hitting the ball with the side of the mallet," Cutter answers.

Graeme nods. "Count the score out loud. Like contact is allowed, mallet to mallet, bike to bike, player to player. No mallet to bike, player to bike, bike to player, mallet to teeth."

The group laughs.

"Throwing of mallets is never allowed," Graeme continues.

The guys shake their heads no.

"Trash talking is always allowed."

The guys nod their heads and laugh.

Graeme puts the round, hard plastic ball, the same type used in street hockey, down on the centerline of the court. The players ride to opposite sides.

Tilly and Camas look apprehensive. Tilly smiles through the nervousness and, while Camas still looks skeptical, she is not about to let her doubt limit her competitiveness.

"Get ready!" Graeme shouts. "Three, two, one, go!"

To the sound of rhythmic rock and roll, the bikes circle each other and the ball. The guys move the ball towards the goal, smoothly passing back and forth to each other. They are skillful and can stop their bikes on a dime to maneuver a turn, or hit the ball.

Tilly is tentative, staying back away from the ball.

Cutter scores.

Camas whoops, "Go Team!"

Tilly's competitive nature is quickly sparked. She rides up alongside Camas to hit the ball and bumps her.

"Hey, foul play!" Camas shouts with a smile.

Tilly continues to ride, drawing on her ice hockey skills to strike the ball towards Josh. He swings and hits the ball skillfully through the goal to score.

"One one," Josh yells.

"Yes!" Tilly shouts, raising a fist to the sky.

Graeme laughs, enjoying the girls' competitiveness and close friendship. Play continues. Ike does some clever bike tricks, wheelies, spinning in place slowly, and a few behind the back shots.

Reeve passes Ike the ball. Ike makes an exuberant swerve to reach it and bumps into Tilly. Tilly falls off her bike and crashes onto the ground. Play stops.

"Brush it off," Graeme says.

"Brush it off, sista," Camas repeats.

"I'm good!" Tilly says, hopping back on her bike.

"Can't win an Ironman if you fall off your bike," Camas teases.

"Can't coach a flea if you're watching my team's bums all game."

They all laugh and play continues.

After the game, the group gathers around a picnic table for lunch on the lawn. Cutter and Joe sit on the grass and Ike, Reeve and Josh stand near the table filled with a spread of sandwiches, chopped veggies, beer and ginger beer.

"How in the world did you learn bike polo?" Tilly asks Graeme.

"Well, as you can see, it's not brain surgery."

"I guess not," Tilly laughs.

"I played during grad school in Seattle for a team called 206. I had a couple of bike messenger friends who started it up there, but it's been around since at least the late 1800s."

"Wow, you are old," Camas teases.

"Not as old as Ike," Graeme smiles.

Ike overhears, laughs and shakes his head.

"What Ironman are you shooting for, Tilly?" Reeve asks.

"I'm not…" Tilly started.

Camas interrupts, "We haven't decided. Maybe Coeur d'Alene in June."

"That's a half. A good goal," Reeve says.

Reeve and Graeme look at Tilly for a response.

She pauses, thinking. After a bit, she says, "I want to do a full Ironman."

"You're just getting started," Camas responds.

The other guys, who have been in conversation, stop to listen.

"What are the distances again?" Camas challenges.

"You know them," Tilly responds firmly.

"Yeah, I just wanted to make sure you know."

"2.4 swim, 112 cycle, 26.2 run. Gosh, Tilly, you're already doing those distances swimming and running. You can do the full," Reeve says encouragingly.

"Thanks, Reeve." Tilly gives Camas a pointed I-told-you-so look. "I'm nervous, but I'm going to do it anyway."

Tilly turns to Graeme, "Here's my why." She takes a deep breath. "I want to send a message for One More Year. I want Liz to make a kit for me that says, *keep your stuff longer, people*. We need to stop all of this crazy overconsumption."

The guys nod their approval.

Tilly continues with a serious look, "I don't want a sponsor. Even if only one person notices and asks what my jersey means, that would mean something."

"Nice," Reeve says.

"Right on," Cutter agrees.

Ike looks proud and gives her a thumbs up, "You go, girl!"

"It will be harder to raise money for what you need without traditional sponsors, but I think we can manage," Graeme says.

"I can put together a training bike for you from some used parts at the shop. You'll need a competition bike, but at least it'll get you training," Reeve offers.

"Thanks."

"Yeah, thanks Reeve!" Camas adds. "Tilly, you certainly do need some meaning in your life since you lost to Captain Camas in bike polo!"

Everyone but Graeme laughs as Camas embraces Tilly. "Love you, sista."

Graeme looks away over the lake. "Let's pack up, gentlemen."

Graeme turns to Tilly, "A good goal for you is Banff in May."

Tilly looks surprised. "OK."

She leans down and hugs Pedro, who has been sitting at her feet, patiently waiting for a snack. She whispers in his ear, "We're going to Banff, big guy."

CHAPTER 24
ANTIQUE MELIOR FRENCH
PRESS WITH BAKELITE HANDLE

The morning light streams into Graeme's bedroom as he sleeps. Roxie jumps onto the bed. He sits up quickly and leaps out of bed in his boxer shorts. "That's right, girl. Let's get to work!"

Graeme pours Heaven's Brothers coffee beans into the grinder on the counter, and the loud noise makes Roxie jump as it does every morning. He pours steaming hot water over the grounds into an old mid-century French pour-over glass vessel and looks out over the lake.

When he sees Tilly swimming, he shakes his head. "That girl sure is committed."

Graeme takes a slow sip of coffee, still watching Tilly. He sets the coffee down and walks to his closet to dress. His strong arms reach down to pull up the cycling shorts Liz made for him.

"Wow, these are so soft, Roxie. Velvet alpaca in my shorts."

Roxie looks away with a little whimper, embarrassed.

"Let's warm up, girl."

With headphones on, Graeme spins quickly on the trainer as he watches Tilly swim. His phone vibrates.

"Hi, Bill."

"Good morning. What are you up to?"

"I'm on my trainer."

"I like it."

"Just warming up. I've decided to train Tilly. I'm meeting her for our first road ride today."

"Terrific!"

"I'm a little nervous."

"What's she riding?"

"Do you remember Reeve?"

"Owns the custom bike shop, right?"

"Yes, great guy. He put a used bike together for her because she doesn't have money for a bike. It's just a training bike."

"Well, if she's any good, you should be able to find a sponsor or two."

"She doesn't want to ride for a sponsor."

"Why is that?"

"She wants to promote a cause instead."

"Well, that would be a first. What cause?"

"I don't know all the details, but it has to do with curbing our overconsumption. She has a clever slogan. One more year. Asking people to keep their stuff longer instead of buying something new."

"Hmmm. Naïve, but interesting."

"There have been some equally naïve ideas that have changed the world."

"Listen to you, all idealistic. He who was mister cynical, only yesterday."

"I know. She's definitely has had an effect on me."

"I can see that. It's a good effect. I might know someone who would sponsor that cause. I can't guarantee it, but I'll make a call."

"Thanks, Bill."

"Graeme, take it easy on her."

"What do you mean?"

"This is not only training Tilly, but you getting back on your bike. Try to remember, it's only a bike."

"That will never be true."

"How are her run and swim times?"

"I know she has endurance because her distances are long. I'll know more about her times soon. I kayaked up to her a couple of days ago and she was so strong. Liz has seen her running."

"How's Liz, by the way?"

"I haven't spoken to her since the dinner fiasco."

"Jackass."

"I know."

"Just apologize and let her know you listened and are training Tilly."

"She was pretty mad."

"Ask her out, please. You and Liz are perfect for each other. You lost her once. Don't lose her again."

Silence.

"Graeme?"

"I've got to run," Graeme says as he spins faster and looks back out over the lake.

"Rox, you need to stay home today."

Graeme leaves Roxie on the dock and starts his boat. As he travels across the lake, a song comes on the radio that makes him think of Liz, and he looks down at his alpaca

94

jersey. He slows the boat to an idle, then turns off the engine. He picks up his cell phone.

Liz is sitting on the front porch of the store, drinking a tea. She answers her phone.

"I'm sorry."

Tilly is standing on the dock with the bike that Reeve built for her, as Graeme arrives.

"I'm nervous about these shoes."

"You should be," Graeme responds.

Tilly looks serious.

"Just kidding. This is our first lesson, and we'll take it easy. You'll have it down in no time."

Tilly and Graeme walk to the marina parking lot with their bikes.

"Pick a foot to be the one you land on each time you stop. I use my right."

"I pick my right too."

"OK, now watch me."

Graeme pushes off, sliding his shoes into the pedals smoothly.

"As you're coming to a stop, well before you stop, slide your right heel firmly out to unclip and then, when you come to a stop, concentrate on making sure your weight is to the right and step down on that right foot."

"I might fall."

"Yes, you might. You'll fall if you forget to unclip or you put your balance to the left over the clipped-in foot. Rest assured, you'll fall at some point, but it will become second nature. Even when it is second nature, we all still have spills from not paying attention. Just make sure it's not into a busy road of traffic!"

"Yikes."

"Let me hold your bike while you practice clipping in and out a few times."

Graeme holds her bike, and Tilly practices putting her shoes in and out of the pedal clips.

"I think I'm ready," she says hesitantly.

Tilly rides slowly through the parking lot, diligently practicing starting and stopping. She becomes smoother and more confident with each attempt.

"Good job."

"Can we ride now?" Tilly asks as she rides past Graeme slowly.

Graeme catches up to her. "Follow me and try to keep the same cadence."

"What's cadence?"

"It's the speed of the rotation of the legs, how fast or slow I'm spinning."

Graeme leads as they ride through the winding roads around the lake for about five miles. Tilly observes Graeme carefully, matching his body and feet positioning as he takes turns and climbs and descends.

"Can we go faster?" she shouts.

"This is our first day out."

"It feels too slow," she says, drawing the words out to emphasize her point.

"Ok, but keep your eye out for potholes, deer, cars passing..."

Tilly pulls ahead and away before she hears the rest of his warning. She starts to build some distance between the two of them, but Graeme speeds up and they take turns leading, riding fast up and down the hills around the lake.

After several miles, they come upon a narrow stretch of roadway. Vehicles slow behind them before passing at a safe distance. A roar sounds from two large logging trucks as they approach from behind. Graeme sees Tilly begin to slow down.

Tilly feels her face flush as she does her best to focus on the painted white line along the right side of the road and ignore the trucks just behind her. She rides the shoulder, careful not to drift too far, which could cause her tire to catch on the edge of the payment and her to fall into the road.

The first truck passes, its draft nearly pushes Tilly over, and the screaming engine smothers the sounds of birds and trees. She sees a pullout and turns into it quickly to stop. She closes her eyes in a grimace and flashes back to an image of a man and a woman riding happily on a lakeside road.

"Are you OK?!" Graeme calls, as he pulls up beside her. He sees her pained face.

"Yes, yes," Tilly takes a deep breath. "I'm fine. Will you lead for a bit?"

"Of course," he says, stalling for a few moments to allow her to recompose.

They ride on, Graeme looking back frequently, and eventually into town to the parking lot of Heaven's Brothers.

Tilly unclips and comes to a graceful stop at the bike rack. "Nice work!"

CHAPTER 25
MOORE DEMONTAGNE 2019 RECYCLED-PLASTIC-WATER-BOTTLE SKATER JACKET

Tilly steps off the porch of her cottage and shivers. She runs back to get a skate jacket designed by her younger brother that she'd found in a Spokane thrift shop. She's dressed in long mountain bike shorts, a T-shirt and sweater. She puts her hair in a low ponytail, then dons her helmet, and pulls on her favorite jacket.

The colorful autumn leaves cover the street and wave to her from the neighborhood trees.

Tilly calls to Pedro. "P, let's go!"

Pedro comes running excitedly out of the house, skidding on the porch.

"Let's go get Cam."

Tilly climbs onto her old school mountain bike, a 1988 Yeti FRO with the chevron paint scheme. Pedro runs alongside through the quaint town of Sandglass to a cottage as cute and small as her own.

Camas is on the front lawn with headphones in. She dances and sings exuberantly, not yet seeing her guests. Tilly laughs and joins her. Pedro, no stranger to dance, jumps up and down on the lawn. Camas is startled when she finally notices them. She laughs, takes one headphone out, gives it to Tilly, and they dance arm and arm until the song ends.

"Come on, slowpokes, we're going to be late," Camas says.

"Nah, we'll be fine if we ride fast."

"Shit."

Camas grabs her backpack and gets on her bike to ride. Tilly pulls ahead.

"Slow down for Christ's sake!"

"I'm in training."

"I just had a cornmeal waffle."

"You ate a big meal before a ride?"

"It's Sunday. I eat waffles on Sundays at The Twisted Kilt. You know, from the bearded dude with the food truck, with the kilt and the waffle iron."

"I'm not stopping when you toss your cookies... I mean waffles."

"I won't if you slow the hell down."

"Just a little. Where are we going?"

"I'm not sure. Graeme only told me that we're going to mountain bike with Liz."

"I thought Liz was mad at him."

"They must have made up."

They arrive at the trailhead to find Graeme and Liz already there, talking and laughing. Roxie quickly spots Pedro and races to kiss him with several licks. They bark playfully.

"Hi, beauties," Liz says happily and gives them both a hug in greeting.

"Girls, can you put a few things in your backpacks?" Graeme asks.

"Sure," Tilly and Camas say in unison.

Liz and Graeme pass them various food items Liz has brought for the picnic. They close up Liz's old Volkswagen van, unload two mountain bikes from the top and strap their helmets on.

"Where are we going?" Liz asks.

"Sherwood Forest... and then a surprise."

"Why are we mountain biking?" Camas asks.

"You know Graeme is always mixing it up," Tilly says.

"That's it. I'm mixing it up." He smiles at Liz.

Graeme takes off first, and the others follow up the trail. The soundtrack of their ride would be an upbeat old school rock song.

"How you feelin', miss waffle?" Tilly turns around to ask Camas.

Camas grimaces. "I'm alright," she says unconvincingly.

After riding for about a mile, several other riders pass them from the opposite direction. As one cyclist approaches, they hear a call, "Tilly?"

"It's Ike!" Tilly exclaims. "Hi, Ike!"

They stop and pull off the trail.

"You're off the boat," Tilly says.

"Yep, need to keep up my skills. They don't call me *love-the-gnarl Carl* for no reason."

"Who calls you that?" Camas asks, skeptically.

"No one really, but they would if they saw my moves."

"If a tree falls in the forest..." Graeme adds.

"Exactly."

They all laugh.

"Nice bike, Tilly. I can see you're the real deal. Not some weight-weeny."

"Thanks, Ike."

"What's new with the logging pricks, Ike?" Graeme asks.

"Graeme," Liz admonishes, nodding towards Tilly and Camas.

"Sorry, girls. What's new with the logging bastards?" he corrects.

Liz rolls her eyes and tries to hide a smile.

"Looks like they're preparing to shut down for the

winter. The assholes don't seem to be doing anything to protect the soil. Once it starts snowing, they won't be able to."

"Maybe Mayor Pat can force them to do some erosion control before the snow," Liz says.

"Maybe... but they haven't agreed to a single request yet," Tilly responds.

"We need to pray it's a dry spring when things melt, or it'll be a disaster," Graeme adds.

"Tilly, I'll see you out on the water. Happy to see y'all," Ike says as he rides past.

Ike puts a flourish on his departure, taking a little curve and the bump below with a loud "yip" and a "yes, ma'am!"

The four smile at their pirate-friend-on-wheels and continue to ride up until they reach the end of the bike trail. They hide their bikes as a precaution against inquisitive bears and continue on foot. Beautiful round cloud formations float below the mid-day sun. Pedro and Roxie run ahead of the group, checking back again and again.

A crystalline alpine lake appears with a sheer granite wall on one side and large smooth, flat and round stones on the other. Snow still covers the top of the granite peak on the edge of the lake.

"This is so beautiful," Liz says to Graeme.

"Not too shabby," Camas adds.

"There's a nice picnic spot over here," Graeme says, as he leads the three to a grassy area between the large rocks.

They sit and each carefully opens up their packs and lay the food out on a colorful, plaid blanket.

"Liz, thank you for bringing all of this!" Tilly says.

"Hey, how do you know that Liz brought it all?" Graeme teases.

Tilly and Camas' hands rise to rest on their hips, and they tilt their heads in a knowing shrug.

Graeme laughs. "Yes, thank you, Liz." Graeme kisses her on the cheek.

"Thank you for inviting me. I feel honored to be a part of this training team. I brought the store's famous homemade cinnamon rolls. Also, some local bacon from Sandglass Butcher that I cooked up this morning and a frittata with spinach, kale, garlic, shallots and goat cheese."

"Yum! Look, I have the beer and some bubbly splits. No wonder my pack was so heavy!"

"Sorry, Camas," Liz says. "I have orange juice too if you'd like a mimosa?"

"I'll stick with beer."

The four enjoy light-hearted conversation about training, hawks overhead, predictions on huckleberry harvest dates, and the tuba player in Camas' favorite band, Handmade Moments. Tilly asks Graeme about his racing days, and he shares a fun story about riding though the Italian Alps with Liz, as they enjoy the delicious food.

"It's warm. I'm going swimming," Tilly says abruptly.

"You'd swim even if it were freezing!" Camas teases.

"You know me."

Tilly walks to the lake and Camas follows. As Tilly pulls off her shorts, Camas pushes her in. Before Camas can get away, Tilly reaches out to grab her arm, pulling her in after her. They both laugh as they bounce up out of the water. Graeme and Liz laugh too, and the dogs bark along from the shore.

Pedro jumps in and swims to the girls, then barks at Roxie to jump in too.

"Go ahead, Rox," Graeme encourages.

She stays firmly rooted on the shore. The girls swim together with Pedro to the middle of the lake.

"Burr, it's too cold," Camas said.

"Swim faster, silly."

"That's what I'm supposed to say to you."

They look up to see Graeme and Liz kissing on the picnic blanket.

"I think we should split this J," Camas says and starts to swim back towards the shore.

They get out of the water a little further down the shoreline. Quietly, they sneak around, pick up the packs, and write a note on top of the beer. "We have the dogs. See you later. Thanks for the picnic!" They head down the path.

"Where did the girls go?" Liz asks, looking around.

Graeme stands up and walks over to where they had gone into the water. He sees the note on the beer.

"Seems they've left us. They have the dogs, too."

"Those matchmakers."

Graeme walks back to Liz and turns some music on from his phone, a slow romantic song.

"Wow, that's quite technologically advanced of you."

"I did own a high tech company, as you may recall."

"That doesn't mean you can operate an iPhone," she teased.

He takes her hand as she stands up. They dance, holding each other close as the fall breeze rustles through the branches of the towering white and ponderosa pines.

CHAPTER 26
BLACK 2016 CARHARTT SINCE 1889 WOOL BEANIE

Camas writes *Training Log* on a thirty-six-inch-wide piece of kraft butcher paper that hangs from a large roll on the wall of Heaven's Brothers café as people in knit beanies with dogs at their feet sit, engaged in cozy conversations. Tilly waves to some friends as she comes in and walks over to sit next to Camas.

"Got you a coffee," Camas says.

"Thanks. What's that?"

"It's your training log. Mick said I could hang this roll of butcher paper, and we can use it to log your progress."

"Not sure I want my progress to be so public."

"What if I allow you a promo spot?"

"A what?"

"We'll ask people to write down possessions they've had for a long time, or maybe things they were going to replace but kept instead. We could photograph them and post them on your OMY website and social media too."

"You've been paying attention, but I don't have a website or social media."

"You do now."

"I do?"

"Yes, princess. You know Benjamin Katz Creative? Well, Ben heard about your cause and put together a site pro bono."

"Wow, that's nice."

Tilly stands up and writes *One More Year* at the top of the paper roll and *keep your stuff longer, people* underneath. Then she adds *Please share what possessions you've had for a long time*.

"Care to get it started?" Tilly asks.

Camas stands up and writes on the paper *Salvo sofa circa 1972, grandma's cast iron frying pan, yard sale 1960's patio furniture. Soul takes time. Triathlete Coach Camas.*

"Thanks, Cam," Tilly says, as she hugs her.

Camas writes, *Tilly headed to Ironman Banff next May* and puts a box around it.

People in the café look over, curious about the wall hanging. A couple stands up and walks over for a closer look.

Graeme runs up the trail to his house. His phone rings just as he gets to the top.

"What."

"That's kind of abrupt."

"Hi, Bill."

"How are you?"

"Great. It's been busy. Tilly's working hard and it's an adventure."

"I saw the article on her One More Year project."

"Yes, she's inspired by that."

"There's someone else who's inspired. The friend I mentioned who saw the article. He wants to pay her expenses at Banff. No product representation required. Just One More Year."

"Really?"

"He's going to email you with the amount available, but I have a feeling it will be plenty. His only condition is that he remains anonymous."

"Any other strings?"

"No. This is a no-strings kind of guy."

"Thanks, Bill. What are you doing next May?"

"I'll be in Banff as it turns out," Bill chuckles.

CHAPTER 27

AJNA ECO ORGANIC NATURAL 2018 JUTE YOGA MAT WITH CARRYING STRAP

Over the days and months that follow, late summer gives way to fall and winter to spring, forming a magnificent mountain montage of strength, sacred stunt rising, and a Sandglass that finds a curiosity beyond skiing, coffee and huckleberries.

Tilly cycles with Graeme along the winding lakeside roads regularly now. They alternate between intense training and slower-paced, scenic rides full of talking and laughing, punctuated with occasional visits from eagles, butterflies and moose.

The Bike Guys have been hard at work for weeks building a wooden frame in the woods, just above the sacred grounds and below the logging project. It would be difficult for an outsider to discern what it is exactly. Still, they use drawings and solid engineering principals and the aesthetics of both bike stunts and tall classic wooden roller coasters, such as the one they have ridden on a sunny surf day in Santa Cruz.

For her running practice, Camas accompanies Tilly from the neighboring village, Beeshoo Ness, along the creek and into downtown Sandglass. Camas spots the Bijou Nez Winery tasting room, which also serves gourmet pizzas, and pulls Tilly inside as they pass. Camas does a double-take on a handsome man's derrière.

Tilly is immersed in Lake Bijou Nez almost every day. She pulls Pedro on the paddleboard as Graeme paddles with Roxie in the kayak behind. Tilly removes the harness to swim faster. Pedro jumps from the paddleboard into the kayak and nuzzles Roxie. Graeme ties the paddleboard to the kayak and follows, looking at his watch periodically to track her progress.

Liz, Tilly and Camas sit in lotus a seated position. Liz and Tilly are motionless, meditating peacefully, while Camas keeps opening her eyes. She is distracted by her shoelace, a butterfly, an itch, a wisp of hair ticking her face. She closes her eyes, then opens one eye to peek at Tilly and Liz, annoyed by their meditating ease.

Tilly and Pedro swim side by side in Lake Bijou Nez, pulling Roxie along on the paddleboard with Graeme and Camas in a motorboat behind. Camas drinks a beer and occasionally blows her whistle.

The Bike Guys and Ike ride bike trails with berms and launch themselves off a few dilapidated ghost mountain bike stunts. They come out at the structure in the woods above the sacred grounds and get to work. They hoist logs with pulleys and a tractor to brace the outside curve of a giant wood frame with a narrow mountain bike track atop it.

Another day, they gather around the back of an old hand-painted pick-up truck that's full of chain netting. They drag the heavy chain across the ground and bolt it to the front of the wooden structure. Snow starts to fall. They cover up their tools and equipment and get back on their bikes. The snow begins to stick and blankets the ground in a magical mountain bike wonderland as they ride together through the woods.

Pedro leaps from Ike's boat and swims towards Tilly. Tilly, wearing a full wetsuit, reaches the marina first and pulls herself up out of the water onto the snowy dock. She pulls Pedro out by the harness, hugs him, and wraps him up in a big towel she had left for them on the dock. Pedro barks as Tilly waves goodbye.

Tilly swims laps in an outdoor hot springs pool surrounded by snow, while Pedro runs back and forth along the pool deck, as steam rises all around them.

Tilly, Camas, and the Bike Guys snowshoe on a steep, mountain trail with the beautiful, snowy vista of the ice-covered lake stretching out ahead of them.

Tilly and Pedro run along a rural road in a valley outside of Sandglass. There are sprouts of bright green growth that peek through the melting snow.

Camas sits at a table at Heaven's Brothers on her Macbook and scrolls through the One More Year social media page to read recent posts. She is pleasantly surprised by all of the activity. She sees a post with a photo of a washer and dryer that reads *1975 Maytag washer and dryer, Jill Reader*, and another, *1968 Lodge Cast Iron Frying Pan, Chap Walker*.

"You go, Jill. Right on, Chappie," Camas says out loud. She clicks over to an online article entitled, *Sandglass Athlete, Tilly DeMontagne, Heads to Banff Ironman*. The feeling of pride for her best friend and the increasing momentum gives her a boost of extra enthusiasm. She looks up to see Mayor Patrick writing on the kraft paper roll on the wall, *1985 21-foot Wellcraft Scarab. 80's boat beetle. Pat O'Connor, Sandglass*.

"That's amazing, Mayor Pat!" Camas blurts out.

He smiles in response. "Well, my wife says I'm cheap, but

they don't make things like they used to, and there's no sense in buying new if she's still perfectly good, now is there?"

"Exactly! And stylin'!"

Camas looks down over the recent additions to the paper and sees a few more entries that warm her heart, including *1984 Subaru Leone 286,000 miles. The lion still roars. John 'Scully' Green, Sandglass.* Just as she is about to look away, a middle-aged woman with short grey hair, wearing cycling attire pays for her Heaven's Brothers Fall Line double espresso, then walks over to the roll and writes *Classic Apple iPhone 3. I miss Steve Jobs. Barb Schumaker, Spokane.*

Camas runs right up to the woman and hugs her to show her appreciation. "Thank you!"

CHAPTER 28

VELDSKOEN 2011 CLASSIC CHUKKA BOOTS

"Liz, this salmon is delicious!" Camas says as she drinks from her wine glass.

She, Liz, Graeme and Tilly enjoy dinner on Graeme's patio two nights before Tilly leaves for Banff. Pedro and Roxie lie at their feet.

"It's from a local Bristol Bay fisherman in town."

"Thank you for this amazing dinner," Tilly agrees.

"Here's to Tilly!" Liz says as she raises her glass.

They raise their glasses to toast.

"It was delicious. Please leave the dishes for me," Graeme says as he gets up, kisses Liz on the cheek, and walks down the steps of the patio.

Tilly follows him. They get onto the trainer bikes in their dinner clothes and start spinning.

Camas starts to follow. Liz holds her arm gently.

"I'm still getting used to this," Tilly says.

"Staying in one place is not your strong suit," Graeme teases, as he looks out over the lake. "I never tire of this view."

"You know, I saw you up at your house before I came to your dock."

"I know."

"How do you know?"

"Because I saw you too."

"Thank you for training me. No matter what happens."

"Thank you for training me too."

"Why did you quit competing?" Tilly asks quietly.

"I... had a bad crash."

"Why didn't you compete again?"

"The easy answer is that it was pretty brutal. A vehicle pulled out in front of me during a town portion of a fast course in France."

"Oh, I'm sorry. Was Liz around?"

"Yes. We had a tiny apartment in Pau, but we parted ways because I was a knucklehead. Then we went to different grad schools and lost touch. I married, went through a divorce, and generally moped around for quite a few years."

"Moping's not good."

"No, it's certainly not. I think that should be a training rule."

"Yep."

They spin for a few minutes without talking.

"I lost my mom and dad a long time ago. Some people get their motivation from a tragedy. I miss them every day, but everyone dies. I don't think my parents would want my life to be about their death. Does that make sense?"

"What should it be about?"

"I'm not sure. Just something else."

Graeme stops pedaling and gets off the bike. Tilly gets down and grabs Graeme in a hug. They walk back towards the cottage and both bend down to pet Roxie and Pedro as the sun sets over the lake behind them.

Tilly and Frida move in slow, flowing yoga postures at the sacred grounds. They are meditative and beautifully peaceful on their mats, overlooking the lake. They flow in unison through several poses, then sit crosslegged, with their eyes closed.

Tilly opens her eyes slowly.

"I think the thing I love most about this place, besides feeling the ancestors with me, is peace rock," Tilly says, gazing over to a large smooth oval stone sitting at the top of a nearby mound. "It gives me hope when hope is hard to see."

Frida speaks lovingly. "That stone was used by the women hundreds of years ago to pound corn and seeds. It is said that they realized the prayers they chanted while working were coming true. Every day they moved it infinitesimally small distances towards the top of the sacred mound where all, but primarily men, would go to meet the ancestors in ceremony and prayer. By the time it reached the top, it had taken more than a year, the woman had stopped using it for food by then and instead used it to make offerings of beautiful sacred objects... a feather, a baby's first lost tooth, a stone, a shed antler, a flower. Dear one, when do you find hope so distant?"

"I see so many useless belongings and that creating them is killing the earth."

"We show by what we worship what we are."

Tilly pulls a cream and brown-striped feather out of her pack. "I found this on my way here. May I make an offering of it?"

"You know the answer to that."

Tilly holds the feather in both of her hands. She takes a deep breath and begins a sweet chant over which Frida's voice coats her in love and protection. Frida lightly cups her hands over Tilly's.

Tilly stands, walks to the peace stone, and kneels. Frida stands behind her as Tilly places the hawk feather gently in the recessed center. She picks up a small twig to hold the offering in place and bows her head in reverence.

CHAPTER 29
RED AND IVORY 1971 VOLKSWAGEN KOMBI BUS MANUAL 4-SPEED

L etera 22, Sandglass' coziest pub and rathskeller, isn't typically open before noon, but Niz, the owner, has hired a band to celebrate Tilly's send-off. Camas, Ike and the Bike Guys enjoy a pint on the front sidewalk. A man in cuffed eggplant-colored canvas pants, suspenders and an open-road rancher short-brimmed Stetson, hand-letters an industrial-enamel *Letera 22* on the window as a local blues duo plays a Muddy Waters cover. People in town who have kept track of Tilly's training, and even those who are just there for the beer, wish her good luck and dance to the music.

"We should get on the road," Graeme says to Camas.

"No beer for you?"

"I'm driving."

"Oh, right."

"Tilly, can I buy you another beer?" Camas asks.

"No, thanks. I think Graeme's ready to go."

Tilly puts her backpack into the back of Liz's van.

"Where's Liz?" Tilly asks, wanting to say goodbye.

"She's inside dancing. I'll get her," Graeme says going inside the pub.

"That guy's a party pooper," Camas complains.

"He's being responsible, I guess. There will be more beer in Canada."

"They drink that horrible piss water. Labatts."

"I bet if a tall, handsome Canadian hockey player offers you a Labatts..."

"Bottoms up!" Camas agrees.

Liz walks out of the pub and laughs as she overhears the conversation. She puts her arm around Camas. "I'm sure you'll find some craft beer in Banff."

Liz turns to face Tilly, "Have fun!" Liz says as she hugs Tilly.

"Break a leg, Tilly!" Josh says.

"Break a leg?" Cutter questions.

"It's a figure of speech from the theater. It means good luck," Josh responds.

"Even so..."

"Thanks, guys," Tilly says as she looks at all of them with tears in her eyes. "I'll do my best."

Tilly embraces each of them, except Reeve, who is at the back of the van helping to secure the bikes. Camas is right behind her and hugs them too in her flirtatious way.

Tilly walks up to Reeve and gives him a big hug.

"Run your own race," Reeve says.

Tilly touches the locket around her neck. "Thanks, Reeve, for everything."

"Where's Ike and P?" Tilly asks.

"He told me he didn't think he could hold it together and might cry in front of P and the guys if he were here. He asked me to hug you for them."

Tilly smiles, gives Reeve another quick hug, then walks over to Liz, who is holding Graeme's hand.

"You know how much I wish I could come with you, but I have to hold down the store," Liz says.

"I wish you could be there too. Thank you so much for lending us your van."

"Of course. You pretend those waters and hills and roads are right here. That they're yours because they are. I'll make sure Burr takes good care of P, and I'll bring Roxie over to see him too."

"Thank you," Tilly says as she hugs Liz.

Liz kisses Graeme and squeezes his hand tightly as he gets into the driver's seat of her vintage Volkswagen bus. Tilly climbs into the back and Camas into the passenger seat. The van is loaded full of gear with the bikes on a trailer in tow.

Tilly looks at the friendly crowd on the street then up to the sky. "The sky's beautiful. Looks like rain."

"Sure does. Lucky we're going to be 300 miles north," Graeme says.

Graeme looks intently at Liz as she stands outside his window, "Don't let Roxie rule the roost."

Liz smiles.

"Stay out of the lightning, gentlemen!" Graeme calls.

"We'll try!" Reeve shouts back.

The van pulls out into the street, and people on the sidewalk call out, "Good luck, Tilly!"

Reeve and the Bike Guys wave, finish their beers, and jump on their bikes. As they ride down the street, they whoop and holler to the thunder, then horse around doing bike polo spins, wheelies and tricks as the lightning streaks through the sky over the lake.

CHAPTER 30

VINTAGE 1978 HANG TEN WHITE NYLON WINDBREAKER WITH EMBROIDERED FEE

"Why don't I swim across?" Tilly asks as they wait in the van for the Kootenay Lake Ferry to arrive.

"It's too far," Graeme responds.

"It's twice the race distance, a total of five miles. I looked it up."

"That's too far."

"I swim farther than that all the time."

"I didn't bring the kayak."

Camas hops out of the van, pulls on her retro navy surfer windbreaker, and runs down to the marina. Graeme continues his argument of dissuasion, but Tilly is not convinced.

"It's too close to the race."

"It's five days away. You told me the training plan. I only need to lay low for the last forty-eight hours."

Camas runs back up to the van. "I found a boat that will follow you!"

"It's dangerous too."

"Don't turn around. I'm changing," Tilly says firmly, as she quickly takes off her clothes to put on her suit and tri-wetsuit.

Graeme abided. "Damn it."

"You aren't mad."

He looks straight ahead at the lake and the large ferry that is just pulling in. "How do you know?"

"Because I've seen you angry before."

"Hurry up. Get out then. The ferry line is moving."

"OK."

"I'll time you."

"See," Tilly smiles as she gets out of the van.

Graeme leaves the van on the parking deck and climbs the stairs to the top deck.

"Look! A person is swimming down there!" an older woman calls out.

People crowd over to the side of the ferry to see.

"It looks like she's racing the ferry."

Graeme looks down at his watch as he times Tilly swimming. "Could very well be."

The woman looks at Graeme and then back to Tilly in disbelief.

"What's the swimmer's name?"

"Tilly DeMontagne. She's swimming to Banff for the Ironman triathlon."

"Go, Tilly!" The woman cheers. The other passengers cheer, "Tilly! Tilly! Tilly!"

Tilly swims strongly. Camas, who sits very close to the handsome young fisherman driving the boat, smiles, and waves like a beauty queen in a parade to the crowd on the ferry.

CHAPTER 31

LEVI STRAUSS & CO 1984 USA OLYMPICS CANVAS DUFFEL BAG WITH BRASS BUCKLES

"Wow, this is cool," Camas says as they pull into Banff village. Dramatic, rugged mountains tower behind the storybook town.

"Just a little ski resort in Canada," Graeme jokes.

"It looks so fancy. Like Sandglass on Aspen," Tilly says, looking out the window.

"Or on Saint Moritz," Graeme adds.

"Does 'ritz' make you swim faster?" Camas asks with a bit of sass.

"Perhaps."

"It could be St. Moritz, Biaritz, puttin' on the ritz, but ritz my ass, they aren't as fast as Tilly."

Graeme laughs and nods in agreement.

"Well, it's stunning," Tilly says, feeling nervous for the first time. She asks quietly, "I suppose we'll eventually find the lake?"

"Yes, we will." Graeme pulls into the hotel parking lot. "OK, girls, let's find our rooms. I want you to rest tonight. No dancing."

"Yes, rest," Camas agrees with her best impression of a serious face. She crosses her fingers behind her back.

"We made it," Graeme tells Liz on his cell phone, sitting on his hotel room bed next to his canvas duffel bag.

"Good luck. It's pouring rain here."

"That's not good."

"You just focus on the race, please."

Rain pours on Lake Bijou Nez. Motored and sailboats come in off the lake and quickly tie up at the town marina. The boats rock from side to side in the lake's whitecaps. People walking down the street rush to find cover under whatever they can find, an umbrella, a magazine, a rain jacket hood. They race to take shelter in shops, restaurants and cars.

A very wet Pedro stands watch from the bow of Ike's boat. Ike ties down tarps over his doors and closes windows. Suerte scrambles into the cabin, soaking wet. Ike calls Pedro to follow him in.

Rain pours at the logging site, and the earth is sopping wet, melting the small patches of leftover snow. The loggers have left a few covered pieces of logging equipment which sit, soaking in mud on the site in an open area of tree stumps.

Frida stands outside of the house in the rain and stares into the forest. Bear leads her back inside.

CHAPTER 32

DANNER MOUNTAIN CASCADE
1991 RECRAFTED HIKING BOOTS
WITH RED LACES

Tilly walks down the street in Banff, wearing a *One More Year* T-shirt over a long-sleeve cycling jersey, hiking shorts, hiking boots, and a small daypack. She passes by the majestic Banff Springs Hotel and through downtown Banff village and is dismayed by the ostentatious displays of consumerism. Large SUVs and fancy sports cars share the street with well-heeled men and women in designer sportswear, splendid shoes and glinting sunglasses.

Tilly steps into a small coffee house to buy a latte and a muffin. As she walks back to the hotel, a woman with short blond hair in a designer blazer, polo shirt, leather tennis shoes, ball cap and large, dark sunglasses suddenly appears as if she making a cameo appearance in a feature film.

"Nice T-shirt," the woman says.

"Thanks," Tilly smiles as she looks down at her shirt.

"I read the article about it. It made me think twice before buying a few things."

"Did you buy them?"

"I did buy this suit jacket... but my assistant found it for me pre-owned. It's Dolce and Gabbana."

"Sweet."

"And the other thing, well, I'm still thinking about it. It's a new car."

"Don't forget that the CO_2 to make a new car just about equals the CO_2 from the exhaust over its lifetime."

"Really? Is that true?"

"Not completely. That road hog jumbo SUV over there uses about four times more."

"Even an electric car?"

"Until we stop making the batteries with coal, nearly."

"Thanks for the reminder." The woman pauses. "It's Tilly, right?"

"Yes."

"I'm Ellen. Good luck tomorrow," she says, as she walks away and takes the hand of a beautiful woman with long blond hair.

As Tilly walks away, she hears someone behind her ask Ellen for her autograph. He asks a second time a bit louder. Tilly feels a tap on her shoulder.

"Excuse me, can I get your autograph?"

She turns around, surprised. "Sure."

A young man hands her a pen and a vintage postcard with a picture of an alpine lake with a small cottage with a deck. Tilly starts to sign the back but stops to read the writing.

"Lake Agnes Teahouse. That looks sweet. Is it still there?"

"It sure is. It's a very popular hike, not far out of town."

"Hmmm. Thanks. Is here OK to sign?" Tilly asks.

"That'd be great. Good luck in the race!"

"Thank you so much. I appreciate it."

Tilly walks back to the hotel where Graeme and Camas are waiting. Camas' hips are moving to a song on her headphones.

"Good morning, sunshine. Let's talk about today," Graeme says, as Tilly approaches.

"Listen to this song! It's awesome," Camas says, as she continues to dance, lost in the music. She hands Tilly one of the earbuds to listen.

"It's cool," Tilly says, dancing.

Graeme is not amused.

Tilly sees his stern face. She pulls out the earbud, then straightens up. "OK. I'm listening now."

"A lot of people are scouting the course. I don't think you need to do that. You'll be able to see the course by following the others tomorrow. Today, I just want you to explore. You can walk around. You can bike or run or swim. My only request, if approved by Camas, is that you limit your total mileage to five. Also, eat Camas-style today."

"Hey!" Camas laughed. "Good advice."

"I'll be getting your equipment ready."

"Do you need help with anything?" Camas asks.

"No, thanks. How about you?"

"No, I think we're all set. We'll see you later."

Camas and Tilly walk away from Graeme.

"Till, I met a cute boy at my continental breakfast while trying to eat enough fried hash browns and greasy sausage to cure my hangover. Mind if I hang out with him for a bit today?"

"I mind the eating of animals," Tilly jokes. "... But of course not. I'm sick of you anyway."

Camas hugs Tilly.

"Go have fun. Just don't forget to hang the Do Not Disturb sign, sexy."

Camas rushes off, and Tilly walks back down the street to fulfill her assignment to explore, without covering too many miles.

"Burr?! What are you doing here?"

"I told my parents that I wanted to watch your race, and they said OK."

"That's so great!" Tilly exclaims as she hugs him.

Burr beams.

"Did you see P before you left?"

"Yep."

"How was he?" Tilly asks, concerned.

"He seemed fine. Ike was playing with him plenty, but I don't think Suerte liked the situation very much."

"Oh, darn. I was worried about that. I hope they're OK."

"Yeah, they're good. Now, he's even better."

Burr's mom walks up with Pedro on a leash, bounding in excitement.

"P!!"

Pedro jumps up and Tilly hugs and kisses him. Burr looks pleased to have helped the reunion. Tilly hugs Burr's mom tightly in greeting.

"I wasn't sure how I was going to do this race without him."

Tilly adds sweetly, "... and you too, of course, Burr. Hey, I get the afternoon off. I'd like to take P out for a bit. I'll bring him back to you this evening so I can sleep without dog breath before the race. Is that OK?"

"Yeah," Burr answers, disappointed he didn't get to hang out too.

"Hey, let's go out on the lake with P when I get back."

Burr brightens.

"P, let's hike!"

CHAPTER 33

1929 CANADIAN PACIFIC RAILWAY ANTIQUE MAP OF BANFF NATIONAL PARK AND THE CANADIAN ROCKIES

"Looks like we're not going over our five-mile limit. Whew, that's good," Tilly says jokingly to Pedro, as she reads the sign at the trailhead, *2.2 miles to the Teahouse.*

The narrow, winding trail to Lake Agnes Teahouse rivals the trails in Sandglass in beauty, except for the steady stream of tourist-hikers of all shapes, sizes, and physical abilities.

Tilly quickly catches her beloved Pedro up on things. "I missed you swimming with me across Kootenay Lake. You would have loved it."

They hike and scamper up the trail together. Tilly's quick conversation is interspersed with the gobbling of snacks and the wagging of Pedro's tail.

"I really wonder if I'll know how to conserve my energy in the race, P."

"Camas told me that she was missing you, even though she would never tell you herself."

"Did Ike take good care of you? I bet you liked the swimming and the rock and roll music."

"I can tell Graeme misses Liz because I catch him looking at his phone, and he never did that back home."

"I've never seen so many fancy watches, furry designer mukluks, personal electronics, or jumbo cross-country rigs. I just don't understand why people need so much stuff, P."

Tilly and Pedro hike and talk, and talk and hike, and snack and hike, and talk and snack. They see remnants of winter snow as they climb the mountain.

"Did you know that 150 glaciers disappeared in the Canadian Rockies between 1920 and 1985?"

Pedro stops, sits, and looks at Tilly. She stops, too, her hands on her hips.

"It's true. And then another 150 glaciers disappeared between 1985 and 2005. That's 150 in sixty-five years and 150 in just twenty years."

She sips from her water bottle and gives him a drink in his travel bowl.

She pulls a vintage Banff National Park trail map out of her pack, opens it and points. "Peyto Glacier is just fifty-six miles from here, and it's lost over seventy percent of its mass. They don't think it will even be around thirty years from now. Where did all the ice go?! Into those ice-melting gas-guzzling Hummers if you ask me!"

Pedro barks in agreement. Tilly realizes her voice must seem loud to passers-by. She leans down to hug Pedro and whispers in his ear, "Listen to me. I was swearing like a sailor and talking as much as Camas too. Sorry, buddy. I'm just really nervous about the race, and I've missed you."

They walk around the next bend in the trail. "Look, there it is!"

Tilly and Pedro walk happily into the Agnes Lake Teahouse and find a seat at one of the few unoccupied tables.

"This is so beautiful!"

Pedro sits at Tilly's feet as she sips her tea and closes her eyes. A breeze blows down from the castle-like, dogtooth, Sawback Rockies, and ripples across the smooth, turquoise lake. Tilly gives Pedro a piece of her scone.

CHAPTER 34

FEMALE CHOCOLATE LABRADOR-MUTT SHELTER MIX WITH SWIMMING GENES AND FETCHING SKILLS

Tilly's cycling shoes, gloves and helmet rest on top of a small towel on the ground as Graeme checks her bike in the swim-to-cycling transition area. He looks up and sees Tilly in her warm-up clothes. Camas arrives and moves the gloves and helmet a minuscule amount.

"She's used to it like this," Camas says, with an authoritative tone.

"That's good, thanks."

"I'm running to check out the start. Get her ready," Camas says as she rushes away.

"Camas will be at the first transition area... and the second and the finish."

Tilly stretches, distracted. "Yes, I know."

"I'll be communicating with her."

Tilly finally listens to Graeme's words and stops her stretching.

"You're not going to be here?"

"No."

"What?" Tilly is shocked.

"It's OK."

Tilly paces nervously.

Further down the lakeshore, Pedro paces with Burr holding his leash.

"OK? How could it be OK.? After all this, you're leaving me now?!"

Tilly paces. Graeme holds her arm in an attempt to stop the pacing.

"Can I tell you something? Will you listen to me? Look at me please," Graeme says firmly, but gently.

Tilly stops and looks at Graeme.

"When I first saw you swimming with P, I said to myself, 'Wow. That girl has power.' I was gruff because you were a mirror of myself at your age. Strong, honest, fearless. It was the very first time I could truly see myself as I was back then."

Graeme pauses. Tilly looks at the ground.

"You don't need me, Tilly. You could have gotten to this Ironman without me. You're a fine athlete and to know this race, and to know yourself, you need to make it your own."

They notice a small group of people have gathered around them and are trying to listen in. A dog barks and Tilly turns to look. She turns back to Graeme.

Graeme continues, "And you have some people to show that they don't need to buy more stuff when they're garage is already full of junk. You know, this planet just may have a chance, thanks to you."

"OK," Tilly answers very softly, a tear in her eye.

"I've arranged for Burr's parents to drive you and Camas home. I'll be staying in close touch with Cam. Get your wetsuit on. They'll be calling you in ten."

Tilly suddenly stands tall and strong. She faces Graeme, holds both his arms, and looks him in the eyes, "Tell me everything, now!"

"OK."

Graeme turns away from the crowd so they can't hear. "Do not let up, not for one moment in your swimming. That's your sport and you need that lead."

"I'm nervous about the crowds in the water."

"We've talked about this."

"I'm nervous."

"Think about P. He has a focus on his target always. He's a water dog. His ancestors in Portugal swam with fishing boats to untangle nets under the water in rough seas. He wouldn't like the big waves, or another boat nearby, or the confusion of nets, but he would have his goal in mind, and he would swim on to reach it.

"Swim on. That's good."

"Yeah, that is good. Swim on," Graeme smiles.

Tilly is still very serious, "What else?!"

"Cycling. I want you to hold back."

"Hold back?!"

"Yes. But it's your decision. You're the boss now."

"Why hold back?"

"You'll have done well in the swim and that will surprise people... your competitors. It will cause them to rev up their cycling. They'll need to catch up."

"But why shouldn't I stay ahead if I can?"

"You can. Certainly, but as we've talked about, there's getting ahead and there's winning. You might consider holding back. They'll think that the swim was possibly all you had. They might go extra hard to catch up with you in the cycling and get a lead, but if you're behind, they'll dial it back too."

"I see."

"Tilly, we've talked through these strategies before. You don't have to worry."

"I want you to know that I love to swim and run, and

thanks to you... fly." Tilly holds her arms out to the side like wings.

"I hadn't cycled in over fifteen years until I met you. I think you're right."

"I don't know if I'll ever do a triathlon again. Will you think less of me if that's so?"

"Of course not, silly," Graeme chuckles warmly. "If I had a daughter, I would wish she were like you."

A loud horn blows, then an announcement crackles over a loudspeaker with a timer countdown and instructions for the first seed.

Camas runs up to them. "Christ Graeme. What the hell? She doesn't have her wetsuit on."

Tilly hugs Graeme, then Camas. Camas is focused on the race and not accepting of the hug. Camas puts a changing tent around Tilly for her to change into her suit and wetsuit and gives her some energy bites.

Graeme smiles at Camas taking charge and walks away into the crowd.

"Get your cap on," Camas orders.

Tilly puts on her swim cap.

"Sista, you go show these god damned oversized Amazons what a Northern-Idaho-woman-of-Native-American-color swims like."

"If I win, will you please stop swearing?"

"Nope."

"Didn't think so."

The announcer's voice comes over the loudspeaker.

"Go! Run! This is your heat!"

Tilly runs towards the lake.

CHAPTER 35
ANTIQUE MOTORCYCLE GOGGLES WITH BAKELITE CUPS, GREEN LENSES AND LEATHER STRAP

A crowd of triathletes in wetsuits wait on the edge of Two Jack Lake. They jump up and down, alternately reaching for their toes and the sky, swirl their arms in airplane circles and talk to fellow athletes as they wait for the race to start. Tilly is in the middle of the herd. She looks nervous as she grabs her locket and looks up to the cliffs of Mount Rundle, which frame the calm lake and stretch high into the sky. The race begins, and Tilly runs with the group into the water until it is deep enough and then dives in. The once still water turns into churning, bubbling, splashing waves as the swimmers exert their power to gain position.

Tilly maintains a steady pace near the rear of the first heat of swimmers. She stops for a moment, feeling a little disoriented, sees Camas on the shore and puts her head down to swim on resolutely. To focus, she rests her mind on Pedro, his webbed paws, his swimming heritage, as her sleek muscles power through the water. Tilly feels the currents and waves of other athletes and tries to keep close to them and on course. She swims ahead of a group of swimmers and follows behind the next pack.

The hour passes quickly as the swimmers round the last buoy for the final leg of the race. Tilly has reached the tail of the lead group of swimmers, all men. She can not easily sense the direction of the now dispersed pack. She looks up to make sure she hasn't swerved off course, finds the finish point on the horizon, and puts her head back down to swim hard. Her breath is steady and rhythmic, with the strong pull of her strokes and kicks driving her forward as she passes a swimmer, then another, then another.

"A female swimmer is covering some good ground. She's passing a lot of female swimmers," a male commentator says into his microphone.

"Don't you mean male swimmers?" a female commentator corrected.

"You're right! They are male swimmers."

Graeme turns the van wipers on about an hour outside of Banff.

Tilly swims to the middle of the lead pack of triathletes. A race referee on the beach looks at his iPad screen. "Can you see that number? Who is that?"

"Number 57!" Camas overhears and calls out, "Tilly DeMontagne."

"Damn. That girl can swim. She's finishing after only twenty men. It's usually about thirty or thirty-five."

The crowd cheers as Tilly exits the water, well ahead of the next female swimmer. She races to the transition area, pulls off the wetsuit to reveal her OMY triathlon kit underneath, then puts on her shoes, gloves and helmet. She lifts her bike off the rack and runs fast through the transition area, jumping on her bike, still in the lead.

Graeme drives through the pounding rain. He sees Camas calling and picks up his phone.

"How's she doing?"

"She won the swim," Camas answers.

"Of course, she did."

"I'm in the shuttle to the transition. I never asked. Why are you headed back?"

"I didn't want to worry Tilly, but Ike called me. He and the boys think the hill's going down today."

"Holy shit."

"It's pouring here and it's worse in Sandglass. Hey, nice work, coach."

"Thanks. Be careful."

Camas continues her ride on the shuttle bus to get to the cycle-to-run transition area. She watches the race on her phone.

"Damn. So much for holding back," she says out loud to herself.

A group of cyclists rides tightly packed at the front of the race, leaving the required distance to avoid being penalized for drafting. Tilly is in fifth place. She looks powerful, bent over her bike, legs spinning, her voice softly humming a Native American song like a mantra. Over the miles that follow, through the wet air, the tune melds into the same melody that Frida sings in the rain just outside her house, looking up at the sky.

At the logging site, rain falls heavily. Water rushes on the ground moving leaves, stones and muddy earth. Trees fall, and a large tractor left on-site begins to slide very slowly in the muddy soil. Animals on the mountain, including birds, chipmunks, frogs, moose, elk and bear, move to higher ground and call out desperately to their forest families.

Graeme calls Ike as he drives over the Long Bridge into Sandglass. Ike is just getting off of a vintage three-wheeler and climbing onto his mountain bike. He wears a sailor-style raincoat and rain hat with old-school, round-rimmed, motorcycle goggles, now known as steampunk from burners and sci-fi literature. Ike opens his flip-phone.

"The hill's going down!"

"How do you know?"

"We can see mud and trees moving down already."

"We have to get those houses below Syringa evacuated."

"I've called the boys. We're racin' there right now. Can you call the Mayor? We'll need help getting people out."

"You got it."

"How's our girl?"

"Not listening to a damn thing I told her."

Ike laughs. "Over."

CHAPTER 36

NEON-COLORED THRIFT SHOP KIDS' SHOCK PROOF 8X21 BINOCULARS WITH BIRD WATCHING CARRYING CASE

Tilly overtakes rider number four as the athletes near the end of the cycling course. They fall back into position, and she makes her move to advance again and pass the rider in third place. The crowd cheers as Tilly and the other cyclists cross the cycling finish line.

Camas starts a chant with her booming voice, "Tilly! Tilly! Tilly!"

The crowd joins in too. A man in the crowd points to Tilly, "What's OMY?"

Another man with long, blond dreadlocks and rainbow, tie-dyed, baggy drawstring pants and T-shirt, looking through neon-colored kids' binoculars, responds in very slow, stoner speech, "I don't know, man. It's not OMG."

"It's OMY, one more year! She's in third place, and she's never even cycled in a race before!" Camas shouts.

"Holy shit, man. One more year? One more year... one more year," hippie-man chants carefully and slowly.

A few others in the crowd take up the new chant, picking up the tempo until the entire side of the course is chanting in unison, "one more year!".

Tilly passes by on her way to the transition area, pauses when she hears the chanting, and smiles. She slows down a bit as she walks by the crowd and a couple of athletes pass her. She hangs her bike in its rack, pulls off her gloves and helmet, pulls on her running shoes, takes a quick drink, pops some hi-tech food pods into her mouth and runs out of the transition area in fifth place again.

"Go, Tilly, I love you, girl!" Camas shouts.

"I love you, girl," hippie dude echoes sincerely.

Camas rides on another shuttle to the finish line area. She answers her phone.

"Camas, it's Bill."

"Hi, Bill."

"Where's Tilly in the ranking now?"

"Aren't you watching?! She finished the cycling section in third place."

"There's almost nothing about her out here."

"I'm picking it up from the race site. Not sure about the rest of the world."

"That's all I needed to know."

"Hey, thanks for the big funds connection. She's still got a marathon to run. Can you help the cause?"

"I'm going to try."

CHAPTER 37

VINTAGE EMBROIDERED BUCKSKIN FRINGED HIPPIE WOODSTOCK JACKET WITH CUPPED METAL BUTTONS

The rain continues to dump down as the Bike Guys race their mountain bikes up the trail to the large wooden structure. The tractor can barely gain traction in the mud to pull up the last available logs to finish bracing *Her Majesty*, as they are fond of calling it after countless hours of building.

Through the mist and rain, the college- and cannabis-engineered log posts brace the elevated track, which hugs the hillside in a firm holding pattern. They quickly finish placing the logs, stand for a few seconds with their arms around each other's shoulders, then look up to admire their work with legitimate concern and a great deal of hope in their hearts.

"Good work, gentleman. Now, we need to hurry down outta here," Ike shouts over the pouring rain. "But it'd be a damn shame not to ride that blessed mother. Calculate the mud!"

Ike takes off first, giving each of the guys a high five as he passes them. Man hugs and more high fives follow as the Bike Guys join Ike. With loud whoops and hollers, they take a muddy lap and climb the impressive structure, swoop down, take the jump at the bottom and ride quickly down the trail to the homes in danger below.

Despite fatigue, Tilly settles into her pace running over moderate hills near lake and mountain vistas. The leaders are within sight. "One. More. Year." She says to the rhythm of her breath.

The rain pours down on the logging site, moving mud, stumps and trees. A striped hawk feather spirals up out of the peace bowl at the sacred grounds floating high into the air.

Graeme drives a lakeside road, headed to Liz's store.

"Damn, this rain," Mayor Patrick says as he answers Graeme's call.

"The hill's going down."

"What?!"

"It's no false alarm. Ike and the boys are there and can see it. They're evacuating Syringa homes. You need to run an emergency announcement, so folks know it's real. Get supplies and the Red Cross going at the fairgrounds. Send your emergency crews over now!"

"I'm on it."

The Syringa neighborhood, filled with small cottages, ski houses, and family homes, lay at the bottom of the hill. The

Bike Guys ride in at full speed, knock on doors and, with forceful urgency, tell residents they need to evacuate immediately. Most grab a few precious things and immediately get into their cars to leave, despite confusion and fear. The guys open their phones to show the mayor's official announcement for those who are skeptical. Many people in the neighborhood know the Bike Guys and give them a hug or shake their hand before they rush into action. The friends on wheels continue house to house.

As the firetrucks, with sirens blaring, drive quickly into Syringa, the fire chief spots Reeve coming out of a house.

"We've cleared out Pine to Treva Street," Reeve announces to the chief.

"OK, nice work. We'll start past Treva."

Cutter hears the sirens, but they have not arrived at the block of houses he is racing to notify. He rides up fast to the next house, knocks loudly, but there is no answer. He bangs loudly again and, finally, the door opens. A pretty, grey-haired, hippy-esque woman in her early 60's, wearing a suede fringed jacket, answers the door.

"I got a call from a friend about leaving my house, but, young man, I don't have a car."

Cutter calls Ike. "Ike, there's a lady here, and she doesn't have a car and..." He turns away and lowers his voice, "she's old like you. I can't carry her, man."

"I'll be right there."

Cutter tells Ike the address then stops to text Camas.

Camas reads the text, *The logging site is sliding. We're getting everyone out.*

Tilly and the other athletes push on as they run through Banff village, now only ten miles from the finish. Spectators cheer. Tilly, in a trance-like state from sheer exhaustion, hears her name being called out and the words *one more year.* As she rounds a bend in the road, she sees Camas with a distraught look on her face before Camas sees her. Camas' troubled face startles Tilly out of her race focus.

Tilly stumbles as she tries to move over to the side of the road to get close to Camas. "What's wrong?" Tilly shouts. "What's wrong?" she repeats desperately, trying to get to Camas.

Camas finally sees her. Incredulous, she shouts back, "What are you doing?! Go! You need to run!"

"What is it? Tell me!"

"Stay on the course. You'll be disqualified!"

"What is it?"

"Nothing! Finish the race!" Camas pleads, "Till, go!!"

Reluctantly, Tilly turns away and speeds up her pace as she runs through the cheering town.

CHAPTER 38

BLACK LEATHER 1971 MILO BAUGHMAN HIGH BACK RECLINER 74 WITH FLIP-OUT LEG REST

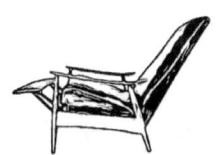

A regal, older gentleman with greying red hair and a well-groomed white beard sits in a modern-style leather recliner, his eyes glued to a huge screen, watching triathletes run along a picturesque road in Banff National Park. The dramatic surf and soft, gentle dunes of the Oregon coastline can be seen through the room's floor to ceiling windows. The man, known as Big Donor to Tilly and Camas, picks up his cell phone.

"Dee, I need you to please get this message from me to Steve Swartz at the Associated Press board, two hours ago."

"Is that the same as yesterday?"

"Yes."

"It's Saturday, you know," she says admonishingly with mother hen care. "And your wife's birthday."

"I know."

"Go on."

"For immediate wire please, Steve: Race finishing within the next hour. Have you caught the Banff Ironman women's race? Upstart Tilly DeMontagne is in third position in the last ten miles of the race. As of a few months ago, she had never even cycled. Tilly is riding for a cause called One More Year. Have you heard of it? She wants people to keep their stuff longer so our planet might have a chance. A good friend of mine once told me that, to change the world, we must first see the world. Tilly DeMontagne may or may not win this year's Banff Ironman, but she is certainly worth watching. Are you watching?"

The room is quiet. The man takes a deep breath.

"Is that it?"

"Yes. Thank you, Dee."

His foot, encased in a Nike shoe, rests on the ottoman. Outside, the sea is crashing in the distance as his wife comes over and kisses him on the temple.

Big donor stands to put his arms around her. "Happy Birthday, dear."

Liz stands on the covered porch and steps out into the rain when she sees her Volkswagen van pull into the driveway. Graeme opens the van door quickly and rushes to meet her on the steps. Raindrops fall on them as they kiss.

Graeme holds Liz close. "Will you come to live on the island with me?"

"Yes."

They kiss and embrace again.

"The hill's going down. Do you have any supplies from the store we can lend?"

"Oh, no! Of course. Let's get them!"

Cutter helps the older hippie goddess put her coat on as Ike races up onto the front lawn riding the three-wheeler. Ike takes her hand gallantly, like a knight from the Roundtable, walks her to his motorcycle, and gets on. She pulls up her long skirt to straddle the bike, puts her arms around him, and they drive off with a roar from the powerful engine and a splatter of mud.

The hillside starts to slide in the rain. Water and debris flow down the hill toward the houses below. The Bike Guys and emergency vehicles rush to get the last people out of their houses.

Ike passes Reeve and the Bike Guys on his three-wheeler as they all look up at the hill and see the trees fall violently, and the earth begins to move.

Frida chants sorrowfully on the porch as Bear, on his horse, reaches down and gently pulls her up off the ground and onto the horse behind him. They ride down the trail towards the water. Frida cries with her head on his back.

Trees, mud, and logging equipment crash down the hill as cars line up to leave the neighborhood below. Debris made up of logs, branches, and stray logging equipment are carried by the water and mud and race faster and faster down the hill. The noise grows louder and louder, as the animals' calls echo in the background.

The large wood structure in the misty woods stands its ground as the crashing sounds of the unforgiving mudslide reach its footing. Debris of all shapes and sizes is caught in the blockade, and ear-shattering creaking fills the air from the force of the mud and trees crashing against the braced wood and the scream of earth leaving what has been its home for thousands of years.

The tons of mud and debris build up higher and higher against the structure and spread out towards the sides. Signs of giving out reveal themselves with progressively louder creaks and wails from strained wood and the twisting of metal bolts and bracing. The flow of water pushes debris around the sides of the structure. A section of the structure finally succumbs to the momentous weight of the mud and busts open. A rapid rush of trees and forest crash through, like air from a punctured bike tire, and blow down the hillside.

CHAPTER 39

HANDPAINTED EST. 1994 LETERA 22 COMMUNITY PUB & RATHSKELLER WINDOW SIGN

Tilly makes her move. She finds a burst of speed from somewhere in the depths of her exhausted body and passes the runner in front of her, who struggles for a time, but cannot keep up.

Camas watches Tilly on her phone and shakes her head, "There she goes."

Camas receives the text from Cutter.

Tilly passes the third-place runner.

Then the second runner.

"Holy shit, Tilly, my girl."

The crowd is chanting along with Camas, "One more year! One more year! One more year!"

"Bring it home, sista."

Mud and lumber crash through the bike men's blood-brother barrier to tear through the ancient earth of the sacred grounds. The peace stone covered in mud finds a resting place in a ravine far below. A hawk cries overhead.

A hawk gives an echoing call over the racers as their aching bodies near the finish line under the silhouette and majesty of the Canadian Rockies. Tilly can hear faint dog barking sounds in the distance which grow louder and louder until she is certain it is Pedro. She can't see him yet, but she reaches down deep into herself to pull the last of her strength from her battered body that has swum miles of Lake Bijou Nez and has run the trails of its mother mountains.

She crosses the finish line.

She passes the cheering crowd and makes her way to Camas and Pedro.

"Why are you crying, silly? You won!!"

"Tell me," Tilly pleads, placing her exhausted head on Camas' shoulder.

Camas holds her tightly. "The hill went down... but the guys and Ike are OK. They saved the people and their houses."

Tilly looks up. Camas looks Tilly in the eyes, "They couldn't save the sacred grounds."

Tilly nods solemnly, then closes her eyes for a moment and hugs Camas tightly.

Camas lifts her off the ground. Tilly smiles when she comes down, turns around and hugs Pedro and Burr. Tilly grabs Camas' hand and Pedro's leash and they walk back through the crowd to congratulate the other athletes. Tilly graciously accepts the congratulations and well wishes from the jubilant crowd.

"They're pretty well set up with beds and food. Got some fire pits and a band playing and donated beer from Letera 22," the fire chief says to mayor Patrick on the phone.

"Glad to hear the stress relief is covered."

"One more thing, Mayor...we found the darnedest thing in the woods."

"What was it?"

"A large wooden blockade of sorts. It looks like that's what saved all of those houses and people in Syringa."

"Well, I'll be damned."

CHAPTER 40

VINTAGE HAWKEYE BURLINGTON GREEN AND TAN WOVEN PICNIC BASKET WITH PIE SHELF

Pedro and Roxie lie on the grass, side by side next to a blanket filled with Graeme, Liz, Bear, Frida, and a magnificent picnic spread of cheese, local charcuterie and wine. With several hundred others, they sit listening to live music from a stage under a large tent at the annual summer Sandglass Festival on the Lake.

The band pauses, and the joyous crowd breaks into loud applause.

Mayor Patrick walks onto the stage and lifts the microphone.

"Hello, friends! Thanks for letting me interrupt this wonderful music. First, I want to thank all of the festival organizers..."

Graeme gets up from the group when he spots Tilly in the crowd, the mayor's voice in the background.

"You didn't hold back."

"Did you expect me to?"

"No, but why didn't you?"

"If I held back, then not only would I have not have done my best, but the others might not have either."

Tilly adds, smiling, "And it would have violated training rule number one."

"Yes, wise one."

"Reeve told me you're still in a lot of pain from the accident."

"I expected someone would eventually."

"Why didn't you tell me things still hurt so much?"

"I think you know. You said it at my house, the day before we left for your race. We may not know the exact reason we do what we do, but it's not about the end of us, it's about the brilliance of us."

The mayor begins to speak again from the stage. Graeme bows respectfully to Tilly, then kisses her on the forehead.

Graeme walks back and sits down on the picnic blanket next to Liz.

"I have a civil service award to present for bravery," the mayor says to the crowd.

Patrick motions with his arm for Ike, Reeve and the Bike Guys to come on stage. The crowd explodes in applause and gratitude as the guys run up onto the stage. They are wearing *One More Year* shirts, all in different colors and styles.

"Hi, gentlemen," the mayor says. The guys acknowledge the mayor with greetings. The noise from the crowd dies down.

"The men you see here risked their lives to evacuate the Syringa neighborhood before our emergency teams could get there."

The crowd stands in applause.

Reeve walks to the mic. "Mayor, can we say a few words?"

Mayor Patrick hands Reeve the mic. "Of course."

Reeve speaks confidently, warmly, "Hey, Sandglass friends..."

The crowd cheers and shouts hellos.

AVIS KALFSBEEK

"Did you hear that our good friend Tilly DeMontagne won her first Ironman race?!"

There is another huge burst of applause. People jump back up and cheer. They look back and see Tilly smiling. Those standing close hug her, give her a high five or kiss her on the cheek.

"Well, turns out, she did that for a reason. You may have seen the One More Year OMY posts at Heaven's Brothers and online," Reeve continues.

The crowd applauds.

"If not, OMY is..." Reeve turns towards the other guys. In unison, they all called out, "One more year! Keep your stuff longer, people!"

There is a deafening round of applause. A band plays low folk acoustic guitar behind the guys as one by one they join Reeve at the microphone. Ike comes to the mic first.

"I'm Ike..."

The crowd cheers.

"...and I've had this guitar for thirty-two years. I hope I get to play with the band tonight. When it needed work, Dan in town, who also makes violins for a living, repaired it."

Dan waves from the cheering crowd.

Cutter steps up to the mic, "Howdy. I've kept my cell phone so far for five years. Larry, at the computer shop in town, has fixed my broken screen three times."

Cheering continues.

Josh steps up to the mic, "I've kept these jeans for six years. My mom keeps 'em decent."

Camas catcalls from off stage. The crowd laughs and cheers.

"I've had my truck for five years," Joe says into the mic. "I bought it used, and it's still used," Joe smiles. He continues, "Stacy over at Hip Stitch sewed cool seat covers for me and, when my car breaks down, which is like... never, I work on it myself."

"Thanks, guys. Let's all..." Camas runs onto the stage, interrupting Reeve. Surprised, he hugs Camas and adds, "Everybody, you may already know her, if not, this is Tilly's coach, Camas!"

The crowd grows even more excited. Camas grabs the mic from Reeve. The band turns up the volume and plays a funky beat to match Camas' dancing. She waves her hand and then opens her palm to face the crowd. The music stops.

"Aren't these the sexiest guys ever, or what?! The Sandglass sexy factor! And we do have it!"

Camas does a slow 360-degree dancing turn, shaking her booty with more music. The crowd dances along too, laughing. Eventually, she stops dancing, and the music quiets.

"This morning in the shower, sadly by myself," Camas says as she looks over at the guys on stage with a flirtatious smile, "... it dawned on me. Simple is sexy."

The crowd applauds loudly.

"If we didn't buy so much damn new stuff, we wouldn't need to carve up mountains for coal to make the stuff, and we wouldn't have to cut down trees to build the ginormous houses to hold that stuff."

Tilly looks tearful as she watches Camas speak passionately.

"I'm not smart, like my best friend Tilly here. I can't outrun her, hard as I try. But I remember what she taught me. And that's getting outdoors instead of getting out your credit card to buy a bunch of crap you won't remember you have in two months anyway. It's killing our planet," Camas said forcefully.

"And to love each other well. She taught me that too."

Camas turns to the Bike Guys and laughs, "Who let me talk so long?!"

She walks over to them and they hug. The band starts up behind them. They walk off stage, arm in arm, waving to the crowd who are all dancing joyously to the happy music.

The moonlight shimmers across Lake Bijou Nez.

Tilly and Pedro walk out of the festival stadium, down a quaint street of small Sandglass cottages, towards home. Some folks who are listening to the festival from their front porches wave a friendly good evening to Tilly.

CHAPTER 41
VINTAGE BULOVA 666 FEET SURFBOARD DIVE WATCH

The lake is as smooth as glass, cut only by the wake of Tilly swimming as she pulls Pedro on the paddleboard. Pedro waits anxiously for his turn to swim.

Tilly sees Graeme's kayak pull up out of the corner of her eye.

She lifts her head to shout, "You're too close!"

The kayak pulls back. Tilly hears a splash, and senses that Graeme is trying to race her. Pedro barks excitedly. Tilly swims faster, but he passes her easily. Tilly swims even harder but is unable to catch him.

Tilly stops, then shakes her head in disbelief as she treads water. "I didn't know you could swim like that!"

Liam, a handsome young man with short curly wet hair and sparkling blue eyes, turns around.

"I thought you were my coach," Tilly says, surprised.

Liam swims back to the side of her board. "Nope. He thought you might want a swim coach."

Pedro barks.

He reaches his hand out of the water to shake Tilly's. "I'm Liam. Graeme's son."

Tilly looks skeptical as she shakes his hand. "Graeme never mentioned anything about having a son."

Pedro barks again.

"So, what can you teach me?"

"Why don't you pass me the harness?"

Tilly unhooks the harness and gives it to him.

Liam motions to the paddleboard. "Hop on."

Tilly climbs onto the board. Liam hooks the kayak to the back of the paddleboard, then swims to the front and fastens the harness to himself.

"First, let's work on some rolling."

"Rolling?"

"If you roll side-to-side like a fish, you'll glide through a large pack of swimmers most efficiently."

"I like that." Tilly turns to Pedro, "See that P, like a fish."

Pedro barks.

"I'll show you."

Liam swims powerfully, rolling back and forth with powerful kicks. He alternately points each of his handsome tan shoulders to the sky as he reaches his cupped hand forward into the water to pull Tilly and Pedro, kayak in tow.

Tilly and Pedro lie down side by side at the front of the board, Tilly's head on her crossed forearms and Pedro's head on his paws, watching Liam swim.

Tilly smiles at Pedro, kisses him on his wet ear, then rests her chin back down.

THE END

PEDRO'S PRIMER

Tilly asked me to share a few words with you. I love her so much, I said yes. Here goes...

I like my kibble dry, not wet, my belly scratched twenty-seven times per day, and playing with my favorite toy, Hedgehog.

Please keep your stuff longer, people. When you go to buy something new, remember *OMY* and the words, *one more year*. Just keep it one more year. And next year, ask yourself the same question.

Oh, one more thing. I like water a whole bunch!

PEDRO DE SOUSA SARAMAGO MEGELLAN

EXTRA FUN READS!

FREE DOWNLOAD

3 SHORT STORY PREQUELS:

Bird-Bully Besties

Lucky Mustard

Giro di Baci

aviskalfsbeek.com/3free

EXTRA EXTRA EARLY
CHAPTERS & BOOKS

FOR EARLY ADVANCES:

——— ◦ ———

Prereleased chapters

Behind the scenes

Pedro planet love

Other writings

——— ◦ ———

patreon.com/pedrothewaterdog

AFTERWORD

"And the response to people who say you can't go back... Well, what happens if you get to the cliff and you take one step forward... or you make a 180 degree turn and then take one step forward? Which way are you going? Which way is progress?"
    Doug Tompkins

www.ingramcontent.com/pod-product-compliance
Lightning Source LLC
Chambersburg PA
CBHW071120100726
47908CB00008B/2444